ONCE IS ENOUGH

ONCE IS ENOUGH

DAVID WRIGHT O'BRIEN

INTRODUCTION BY
John Gregory Betancourt

WILDSIDE PRESS

INTRODUCTION

David Wright O'Brien (1918–1944) was an American writer of science fiction, fantasy, and mysteries—primarily short stories. A nephew of Farnsworth Wright, the legendary editor of *Weird Tales*, O'Brien was just 22 years old when his first story ("Truth Is a Plague!") appeared in the February, 1940 issue of *Amazing Stories*. Because of the high quality of his writing, and the war-time scarcity of young writers, he became one of the contract authors for the Ziff-Davis chain of magazines, which included not only *Amazing Stories*, but *Fantastic Adventures, Mammoth Detective*, and many others. Between January 1941 and August 1942, he had more than fifty-seven stories published in magazines, most of them written under the pen names John York Cabot, Duncan Farnsworth, Clee Garson, and Richard Vardon. Some of the stories were co-written with his close friend William P. McGivern, with whom O'Brien shared an office.

He continued writing even after he enlisted in the U.S. Army Air Force during World War II, adding "corporal" before all his pseudonyms. He died at age 26, shot down while flying a bombing raid over Berlin. But for this tragic end, I have no doubt that he would have had a stellar career as a writer of not just fiction, but motion pictures and television shows, much as McGivern did.

Wildside Press published a collection of some of O'Brien's best science fiction and fantasy work, *The David Wright O'Brien MEGA-PACK®*, in paperback and ebook in 2019, selected and edited by Von Rothenberger, who has become O'Brien's leading authority in recent years. Hopefully this volume will continue the trend of bringing this lost author's work to modern readers.

This story was originally published in the November, 1943 issue of *Mammoth Detective*.

—John Gregory Betancourt
Cabin John, Maryland
June 29, 2020

CHAPTER I

As consciousness returned to him, Thane fought to push aside the thick curtain of nausea and pain which blanketed his mind. Somewhere in the distance a telephone was ringing with evenly spaced insistence, and Thane tried to struggle to his feet to answer it.

The sickening vortex of blackness was resolving itself into thin wispy fragments of fog, and light stabbed blindingly into Thane's eyes as he opened them.

"A minute...jus' minute," Thane mumbled thickly.

He managed somehow to push himself upward on his elbows. The ringing was louder now, and more insistent. Thane shook his head from side to side, trying to clear the last of the fog wisps from it. Pain lanced molten shafts of agony into his temples and he groaned, clutching tightly to the cool, hard object in his right hand.

The whirlpool of light and pain and sound no longer engulfed his senses, and for the first time he was able to bring things into focus.

The telephone still rang.

"A minute—" Thane began.

And then he saw the gun. It was the cool, hard object he clutched in his right hand. Instinctively his fingers released it, and it thudded softly to the thick brown carpet.

Thane managed to rise, now, even though the effort was measured in cold-sweated sickness. He caught the edge of a davenport and held fast to it while some degree of balance and strength returned to him.

The ringing of the telephone jarred him again, its clamor not to be denied; and Thane released his grasp on the davenport, taking an unsteady step in the direction of the sound.

He almost stumbled over the body.

Thane's choked horror wheezed in his throat, his eyes dilating with shock and terror.

The body was that of a man. It lay face forward on the thick brown carpet, one arm thrust rigidly forward holding a wrought-iron fireplace poker. The tip of the poker was stained, sticky with browning blood.

The telephone had stopped ringing.

Thane's eyes went to the gun he had dropped. It lay less than a yard from the dead man's hand. In the terrible silence that was louder than noise, Thane stared ashenly at the body.

Tearing himself from the hideous fascination for the corpse, Thane looked around the room.

Large, spaciously ceilinged, expensively furnished, it was obviously the drawing room of a lavish apartment suite. A wood-burning fireplace in the far center of the room, displaying ashes and charred fragments of birch, snapped Thane's mind back to the blood stained poker in the dead man's hand.

To his right, before another davenport, Thane saw a low, stump-legged cocktail table on which two glasses stood beside a whisky decanter, a siphon bottle and a bowl of ice.

One of the glasses was clean, obviously unused.

Thane closed his eyes, his teeth biting hard into his underlip and his nails digging deep into his palms while he fought for control and some semblance of reason.

His need for control was desperately urgent. Thane had never before in his life been in this room. He had never, at any time in the past, known this man who now lay dead upon the floor. Thane had utterly no idea of where he was, or how he had gotten there.

Thane opened his eyes and fought away the momentary dizziness that surged through his aching head. Steadying himself again on the arm of the davenport behind him, Thane gingerly touched the swollen wound on the right side of his skull above the ear.

His hand came away sticky with darkened blood and matted strands of his own dark hair. His eyes returned to the stained, sticky tip of the poker in the dead man's hand. With sickening certainty he knew that similar strands of his dark hair were clinging to the bloody end of that poker.

Thane fought back the panic that swelled in his chest. He tore his eyes from the poker and forced himself to stare at the body.

The dead man was dressed in a blue smoking jacket, gray, pin-striped trousers, and slippers. He was about Thane's size and build, perhaps an inch shorter, four pounds lighter—approximately five feet ten inches tall—weighing around a hundred and eighty.

His gray hair indicated that the dead man was from ten to fifteen years older than Thane, however. Somewhere between forty-five and fifty.

Thane forced himself to step up to the body, to bend forward while he gently, very gently, turned the dead man's head to the side.

It was difficult, almost impossible, to tell what he had looked like. Several bullets had shot away a considerable portion of his jaw, and blood smeared the rest of his features. Thane was able to see, however, that the man had a gray mustache, a straight, aristocratic nose, bushy gray eyebrows. His forehead was surprisingly low and wide.

Thane moved the head back to the position in which it had been lying and straightened up.

Cold sickness came even more strongly to Thane, and his forehead shone with sweat. He turned and stumbled across the room to a window. He threw it open, the effort bringing the cold sweat out in torrents.

Thane leaned out the window and found himself staring down some fifteen stories into a darkened alley below. He began to vomit.

Several minutes later Thane pushed himself back from the window sill. His face was even more ashen than before. But some of the nausea had left him and the green circle around his mouth was gone. He went over to the stump-legged cocktail table, took the clean glass and the decanter, filling the glass with four fingers of whisky.

He gulped this down with a single back snap of his head. He shuddered deeply, then, putting the glass and the decanter back on the table.

The whisky warmed him, steadied him.

The telephone began to ring again.

Thane looked up in the direction of the sound, a hallway at the other end of the drawing room, a hallway several yards beyond the body of the dead man.

The telephone rang four times before Thane reached it. He picked it up from its cradle, put it to his ear. He made his voice a thin mumble.

"Hello," he said.

There was the definite sensation that someone was on the other end of the wire, and yet no voice answered him. After a moment a click told him that the other party had hung up.

Thane put the telephone back in the cradle, turned back toward the drawing room, and saw his hat and coat.

They were lying carelessly atop a hall table below a mirror. His pigskin gloves were atop his fedora, the fedora atop his brown polo coat.

Thane looked at them a moment, then went back into the drawing room. He passed the body of the unknown murdered man

9

quickly, not looking down, crossing the strange room to a door at the far right end.

The door was ajar, and Thane pushed it back further, stepping into a small hallway bordered by three other doors, one of which was open.

The open door revealed a washroom. Thane entered it, stepped over to the washbowl, turned on both faucet handles, found some soap, and mechanically began to wash the blood from his hands.

Hands washed, Thane removed his suitcoat, searched it for bloodstains, found none, and removed his vest. His vest was also unstained.

Thane found a towel, opened his collar and inserted it, bib-fashion, to cover his neck and shoulders. Then, with another towel, he began the painful task of washing the wound on his skull.

The wound had stopped bleeding, and Thane cleaned around it, gritting his teeth against the pain. When he had finished he turned the hot water tap on full, rinsing the bowl of blood and dark hair. He rolled the soiled towels in another larger one which was clean. Carrying these, Thane went back into the drawing room.

Thane stopped by the cocktail table, picked up the glass he had used and the decanter, and started to smear what prints there might be on them. Then, in recollection, he turned to the window he had opened.

He cursed then, staring around the room desperately. He put the decanter and glass back on the table. It was no use. He didn't know where his prints might be found. They might be everywhere around the place, and there was no way of being certain.

He started toward the body on the floor, then stopped, cursing again. There was no sense in cleaning the poker, no sense in smearing prints on the gun, for the same reason.

Thane began to tremble. Panic surged again in his breast, and this time there was no denying its command. He was trapped. In a room with a dead man—a man he, Richard Thane, had to all evidence murdered brutally.

Trapped in a room he had never in all his life seen before. Trapped with the body of a man he had no recollection of knowing. His mind reeled and sickness began to flood him again in cold, sweat-washed waves.

Thane was still carrying the rolled towels as he made for the hallway in which he had seen his hat and coat. He left them beside the telephone as he struggled into his coat, picked up his hat and gloves.

10

They were still beside the telephone as Thane stepped out of the door and into a long, carpeted hallway....

* * * *

The time in which Thane left the building had passed in a blur of panic to him. He remembered that there had been an elevator at the far end of the hallway—and he remembered deciding against its use while he stumbled to the other end of the corridor and found the stair exit which had been marked by a red safety bulb above the door.

He had stumbled dazedly down endless flights of stairs, his breath searing his lungs and the cold sweat of panic drenching his clothes. He had thought at several times that he was about to collapse. And finally there was an exit light on the ground door. Cold air had engulfed him chillingly as he staggered out into an alley, and a thin mist of rain blew into his sweat-streaked face.

Thane had followed the alley, then, and the alley had led him into another until he at last found the courage to step out into a street.

The panic had left him now, to be replaced by a dull, numb horror. The street along which he walked was in a quiet residential section, and, save for an occasional car passing by, was utterly deserted.

Thane heard the streetcars rattling along the tracks, and the hum of a steady, fairly heavy traffic at the sudden termination where the little street joined a boulevard half a block ahead of him. It was only then that Thane began to realize where he was.

The familiar lines of the buildings on the corner ahead, the lamp-lighted precincts of the small park on the far south side of the street, the rattling surface cars half a block beyond that, told Thane—even before he recognized the Newberry Library—that he was approaching Bughouse Square.

He slowed his walk, stopping to peer at his wrist-watch. It was 1:10.

Thane thought suddenly of Lynn.

Lynn was Mrs. Richard Thane, his wife.

"Chow mein—and don't, please don't, forget the eggroll," she had told him. How long ago was that? Thane thought, while the hot lances seared his head. It was ten after one. He had called Lynn from the office at five o'clock that afternoon. Eight hours.

"You can expect me about six-thirty, then," Thane had told her. "I'll call Old Cathay and have them get the stuff ready. I won't forget the egg-roll."

11

"I'll stir up a nice tall shaker of Martinis," Lynn had promised.

Thane remembered leaving the office. It couldn't have been later than five-fifteen. His office was on LaSalle, directly across from the City Hall and County Building. He had looked for a cab and hadn't been able to get one immediately. He'd walked south to Washington and stood there on the corner trying to signal one. Then he had remembered that he'd forgotten to telephone Old Cathay for the food.

There'd been a small bar, one Thane patronized only infrequently, but a nice enough little place.

He had decided to have a before-Martini-before-dinner Scotch and make his call to Old Cathay from there. Thane tried to remember the place. He couldn't think of its name, although its location and appearance were easily remembered. Nothing pretentious. A bar, with booths and tables in the back and to the side.

Thane had gone into the bar, ordered his Scotch, and asked for a slug with his change as he paid for the drink.

The bartender was an amiable, moon-faced, bald little man, and had pointed out the telephone booth in the back. Thane had tasted his drink, put it down, and gone back to call Old Cathay. He tried, now, to remember what customers were at the bar.

Not more than four or five. Two women and a man at the front end. A couple in one of the rear booths. No one at the far end of the bar where he'd left his drink.

Thane tried desperately to remember the details accurately. There'd been another customer at the bar. He felt certain of that. And yet he couldn't recall it clearly. Suddenly he realized why. The other person hadn't been at the bar until Thane came back from making his call to Old Cathay.

He took a seat several minutes after Thane had almost finished his Scotch. Took a seat to Thane's right, in front of a glass that Thane hadn't noticed until then.

Thane recalled, now, that he had scarcely noticed the man on his right. He was unable to recall anything of the other's appearance, and realized that he must have looked at him in the unseeing, abstracted fashion in which one commuter glances at another—gathering no impression whatsoever.

Now Thane stopped, standing on the corner. Several cars went by. An army truck passed, followed by a sports roadster. Half a block off, a northbound Clark Street car rattled noisily along.

Thane was frowning now, temporarily lost in his effort to recall what had happened in the bar after that.

His memory went no farther.

Thane wiped the rain and sweat from his white, strained face with a gloved hand. He was beginning to tremble again. What had happened after that? What in the name of God had happened?

Eight hours had passed since then. Eight hours—seven and a half, at least—which were an utter blank to him.

Thane dug his hands deep into his pockets, jamming his knuckles roughly down on a package of cigarettes. What had happened in those eight hours?

He had murdered a man.

"No!"

Thane clenched his fists even tighter in his pockets as the word rang desperately in his mind.

"No!"

He had murdered no one. He remembered the gun that had been in his hand when consciousness returned. He remembered the ugly mess the bullets from that gun had made of the murdered man's face. He remembered the poker, with Thane's blood and Thane's hair on the end of it, gripped in the dead man's hand. He remembered all this and pushed it desperately from his mind. He was not a murderer. Richard Thane was not a murderer.

He had to believe that.

CHAPTER II

Thane found an all-night drug store on North Clark Street some five minutes later. He had decided by this time that he had to call Lynn.

The decision hadn't been easy to make. The thought of involving his wife in the terrifying chain of circumstances which had enmeshed him during the past eight hours had been almost more than he could bear to face.

He had realized, however, that the risks of such a call as balanced against the necessity were slight. It had been no more than fifteen or twenty minutes since he had left the apartment and the murdered stranger, Thane estimated, and the chances were strong that the police might not discover the body for some time.

Too, after the discovery of the body, it would be several more hours, perhaps considerably longer, before the evidence leading to Richard Thane—the evidence in the form of prints and other laboratory matter—would be sorted. The prints would be the most damaging evidence, Thane realized, inasmuch as he had been fingerprinted more than a year ago on a passport matter for a short South American trip he'd taken. Sent to Washington by the local police, the prints picked up in the murdered man's apartment would—in a matter of hours—be checked against those on file in the Bureau of Fingerprinting and Identification. By return telegraph the most damning of those prints would be identified as belonging to Richard Thane.

But until that time, Thane would not be hunted. That gave him temporary freedom. A freedom measured in hours.

Thane asked a busy drug clerk for a slug, reached into his pocket, and realized he had no change. He brought forth his bill fold and was reaching into to find a dollar when he saw the thick, crisp sheaf of bills there.

At the time that he had left his office, over eight hours before, Thane had had something under twenty dollars in his wallet. It was used, crumpled currency, none of it fresh, and had been, he recalled, in denominations of five, ten, and some singles. The five and the ten and one single had not been touched. The other bills had been added to it during those blacked-out hours.

Thane saw the drug clerk staring at him impatiently, flushed, and pulled forth a single, hastily closing his wallet and dropping it into his polo coat pocket.

He took his slug and ninety-five cents change and went to a telephone booth in the rear of the store.

Inside the booth, facing the telephone, his back hiding his inspection, Thane took the wallet from his pocket and counted the crisp notes.

There were twenty-five of them. Each was a hundred dollar bill.

Two thousand five hundred dollars in crisp, fresh banknotes! Thane's hands trembled badly as he put the money back into the wallet and the wallet back into his pocket.

He had to sort through his change twice before he found the slug, and he made two mistakes in dialing the number of his apartment before the call was finally put through.

There was a momentary, far-away crackle in the connection, then the buzzing began to indicate that the operator was ringing the call.

As the moments passed and the regularly spaced buzzing continued, cold perspiration came again to Thane's forehead. Lynn should have answered almost immediately. There was a telephone in their hallway, right off the living room, if she were sitting up, and another connection beside the bed, if she were sleeping.

The operator broke in after several minutes.

"They do not answer. Shall I keep on ringing?"

Thane put the receiver back on the hook and the slug clanked noisily down into the return slot. Thane opened the door of the telephone booth and stumbled out, almost bumping into a counter displaying alarm clocks and electrical accessories.

He moved through the drug store and stepped out into the street without being aware of the several customers who stared curiously at his ashen-faced, lurching figure. He didn't hear one of them remark:

"He's either hopped up or gin-happy."

Outside the drugstore, Thane turned south, toward the Loop, and started walking. It had stopped raining and the breeze was cold on his face. The noises of Clark Street at night were all around him. People who passed, and drunks who sometimes jostled him, were unnoticed.

Lynn was gone. Lynn wasn't at their apartment. Lynn, wild with anxiety, perhaps, or merely angry at what she might think to be a stand-up resulting from a thoughtlessly impulsive spree, had left the apartment.

But where had she gone? Where would she go under circumstances such as this?

Thane tried desperately to think.

If her anxiety, worry, had been the cause of her leaving the apartment, she would undoubtedly have intended to search for him, to call his friends, perhaps, in an effort, to learn if they had seen him. But she wouldn't, Thane realized, find it necessary to leave the apartment to make telephone checks at the places he might conceivably be.

Thane knew, too, that should the other alternative be the case, should she be angry and certain that he had sallied off to a round of bars with some friends accidentally met, it was more likely that she might leave the apartment. Perhaps, disgusted, she had gone to a friend's home to spend the night. Mentally, he checked a list of Lynn's closest women friends, then decided that it would be completely out of character for her to advertise any domestic strife to her friends by such a move. No. It wasn't likely that she'd spend the night at any one of their apartments.

Of course there were numerous other possibilities. Perhaps some friends of theirs had dropped in at the apartment during the evening. If Lynn had been angry, rather than worried, and the friends had planned to ask the Thanes to go out with them night-clubbing, it seemed reasonable to assume Lynn might—figuring to hell with him—have gone along with the other couple.

It was incredible how many other plausible explanations there were when you started thinking of them. Realizing this—though also realizing that he might be guilty of wishful thinking in regard to such explanations—Thane forced himself back into the somewhat numb composure he had had a few minutes before calling Lynn.

There would be nothing he could do about reaching Lynn now. Nothing whatsoever. He could call again shortly, and again after that if it were necessary. For the present, he didn't dare go to the apartment. And, too, for the present, he had to straighten himself out; had to get a grip on his sanity and his stamina. Quickly.

Liquor helped a little.

Three double-Scotches obtained at the next saloon he came to, did much to starch Thane's senses and courage. The whisky warmed him and dulled the ache in his head. He was able to think a little more clearly.

* * * *

He was steady when he left the place. Much more steady than he had been when he entered. Thane had heard of men being in the state where no amount of alcohol could make them drunk, and until now had always believed such stories to be beyond the realm of physical possibility.

As he stepped out of the saloon he was able to catch a cruising taxi immediately.

"La Salle and Washington," he told the driver.

Settling back, Thane found himself wanting a cigarette for the first time since his return to consciousness in the strange apartment. He pulled out the badly damaged pack and lighted a smoke with hands that trembled surprisingly little.

He had finished half of the cigarette, four minutes later, when the driver stopped at the intersection address Thane had given him.

Thane got out of the cab, paid his fare, and started up the block in the direction of the tavern which, over eight hours before, he had entered under such utterly different circumstances....

The place was named The Idle Moment, Thane observed from the window sign. He entered the tavern, and noise, laughter, shrill voices in conversation and the music of a juke box playing Black Magic swelled around Thane as he stepped through the door.

For a moment Thane stood there impervious to the babble and confusion, his eyes searching the other side of the bar until he found the moon-faced, amiable little bald man who had been the only bar-tender on duty that afternoon.

The moon-faced little barkeep had his post at the far end, and Thane moved along the bar toward him, searching for an empty bar stool.

Several stools were vacant down there, and Thane moved onto one. A blonde to his left giggled and winked at him.

"Hello, big-boy," she smirked.

Thane ignored her; and then the moon-faced little barkeep was coming up to him, his face professionally bland.

"What'll you have, sir?" he asked.

Thane placed a five dollar bill on the bar, and forced a grin.

"Something a little easier on me than what I had early this afternoon," he said.

Sudden recognition came into the bartender's eyes.

"Say!" he exclaimed. "You're the fella who took sick so sudden this afternoon! How you feeling now? What was the matter?"

There was nothing in the bartender's voice, Thane decided, but genuine surprise and interest.

"I'm feeling much better," Thane said.

"Lucky thing your friend happened to be on hand," the barkeep said.

Thane's heart skipped a beat.

"My friend?" he asked casually.

The bartender looked puzzled.

"Sure. Didn't he take you home? He took you out of here."

Thane forced himself to grin ruefully. "I wondered how I made it to a cab and got home," he said. "You know, I haven't the faintest recollection of leaving here. In fact, I didn't know a friend of mine was here. Did he come in after I got woozy?"

The bartender grinned, scratching his bald head. "Come to think of it, now, he was sitting in the dark in a back booth when you came in. Then, when you went to make a call, he came out of the booth and brought his glass to the bar with him. Took the stool next to yours."

"Yes?" Thane said. "That's interesting. I wonder if it could have been—" He hesitated, then added, "But go on."

The barkeep rubbed his bald head again, reflectively. "I think he just put his glass on the bar. Anyway, when I saw him a minute later, he'd turned away and was starting toward the back. I thought he was gonna knock on the door of the phone booth to get your attention, but I guess he went to the washroom instead. You came out of the phone booth a minute later and sat down and started to finish off your drink. I remember I started polishing some glasses, and the next thing I know you're sick as a dog and almost out cold. This guy has come back and is standing beside you, helping you to get off the bar-stool."

Thane's heart was pounding rapidly in excitement. He fought to keep his features composed, to keep his voice from shaking as he asked:

"Did he say anything?"

The barkeep nodded. "Yeah," he rubbed his chin. "Yeah, he said—"

"Hey! You gonna gas all night, or are you gonna wait on customers?" a shrill voice on the left rasped.

Thane and the barkeep turned to see the blonde pounding her empty glass on the bar while she and her escort glared angrily.

"Okay, okay," the barkeep said wearily. "What'll you have—the same?"

He nodded apologetically to Thane.

"Just a minute," he said.

Thane's nails bit into his palms as he clenched his fists in rage. But he kept his expression drained of any emotion, forced himself to light a cigarette from the glowing stub of the one he'd been smoking.

It was an effort to hold his mind in rein. His thoughts galloped in every direction, wildly stampeding at this first, tangible information that had come his way. He had been drugged. Drugged obviously by something placed in his drink when he was in the booth, telephoning.

The man who had drugged him had slipped the stuff into the drink while Thane was in the telephone booth, left his own glass near Thane's, and gone to the washroom until he heard Thane emerge from the booth. Then he'd waited long enough for Thane to drink enough from his glass to start the grogginess. He had returned to the bar just as Thane was near collapse, with the intention—which obviously had worked—to get him out of the place under the guise of a good Samaritan.

Thane steadied his suddenly trembling hands against the bar. It was obvious, utterly obvious, that the man the barkeep was telling him about was the same one who had arranged the incredibly fantastic murder frame-up in that luxurious apartment.

The same hands that had helped Thane from the bar-stool and out into the street, were undoubtedly the same hands that had slain the mysterious man in the strange apartment. The same hands that went to work, then, in a cunning and incomprehensible motivation designed to start Thane on his way to the electric chair for murder.

The moon-faced barkeep returned to Thane now.

"Those damned broads," he grumbled, "are enough to make a guy get outta this—"

Thane nodded impatiently.

"You were just about to tell me what my friend said as he started to help me out," Thane prompted.

"Oh. Yeah, that's right," the barkeep said. "Like I was telling you —you was almost out cold. This friend of yours says you musta been sopping it up all day, and I said that was funny, since you didn't show it none when you came in. He says you never show it until you get sick and start to pass out. Anyway, he's a friend of yours, like he tells me, and he oughtta know, I figure. He helped you out the door, his arm around your waist. You wasn't walking so wobbly, but your eyes was sure glassy. I guess, then, he put you inna cab, like you say."

"He didn't come back into the tavern?" Thane asked, though he knew what the answer would be.

The barkeep shook his head. "No. That's how I figured he took you alla ways home."

Thane nodded. "That's certainly funny as hell. I don't remember anything until the cab pulled up in front of my house. I came around enough to get out and get upstairs. I wonder who my friend was? Maybe it was—say, what did he look like?"

The bartender rubbed his bald head, irritatingly deliberate. He frowned, pursing his lips and cocking his head. Then he glanced at Thane.

Thane went through a hideous eternity of suspense in those brief seconds. Supposing the description proved to be that of a friend of his, actually? Supposing, as he suspected it would, it would prove to be that of someone utterly unknown to him? In either event, Thane felt grimly positive that it would be the description of the person who, through cunning, mysterious malevolence, had determined to frame him for the murder of an utter stranger.

"Well?" Thane demanded.

"S'funny," said the barkeep. "Best way I could describe your friend would be to say he was about your size, maybe an inch or so shorter. About your weight, too. Yeah, a build pretty much like your own. He had gray hair, though, and he had a gray moustache, and, oh, yeah, a nose real straight and, ah, dignified looking."

Thane stared speechlessly at the moon-faced little barkeep. He felt a fresh wave of sickness and bewilderment and fear sweeping over his brain and body. The man the barkeep had described was undoubtedly the murdered stranger in the swank apartment; the stranger who'd been slain by the gun Thane had found in his hand; the stranger who'd held in his death-frozen grasp, a poker sticky with Thane's own blood!

CHAPTER III

It was fully a minute before Thane realized the barkeep was staring at him curiously.

"Whatsa matter?" the bartender asked, misinterpreting the expression on Thane's face. "Was the guy I just mentioned your boss, or something?"

Thane forced a smile.

"No," he said quickly. "No. Nothing like that. He was just a very old friend I haven't seen for a number of years, that's all."

"Well, can you beat that?" the barkeep observed with rare philosophy. "It's certainly a small world, ain't it?"

"It most certainly is," Thane agreed. "Supposing we have a drink on it."

The barkeep shook his head solemnly. "Gave the stuff up twenty years ago, thanks. Poison. Take a cigar, though."

"All right," Thane said automatically, "and bring me a double Scotch. You can skip the wash."

Four minutes later Thane left the tavern. On the sidewalk, he hesitated. The rain had started again, more heavily than before. He turned up his collar, found his cigarettes, lighted a smoke. Then he started east along Washington.

At State Street, Thane turned north, after crossing the street, and at Randolph went into the big Walgreen's on the corner there. He got a slug from the cashier at the cigar counter, rode the escalator down to the basement, and found a vacant telephone booth.

Inside, he hesitated for a moment, unconsciously holding his breath, before putting the slug in the slot. Supposing she still was not at home? He glanced at his watch. Five minutes after two.

He dialed his number rapidly.

The waiting was again an eternity of suspense. And again, when the established interval of buzzing had passed, the operator broke in to ask him if he wanted her to keep on ringing. Thane hung up wearily.

Where could she be? He was much more worried than before. Suppose something had happened to her. Suppose she had, somehow, been involved in this terrible thing by the same maliciously cunning forces that had involved him.

The thought had been with Thane all along, ever since Lynn came to his mind. This was the first time that he had permitted himself to consider it.

Supposing Lynn were, at this moment, involved in the terror and trouble he faced.

The supposition called for considerably more rational consideration than Thane had given it. But Lynn was involved, not he, in its hideous potentialities. He could no longer be rational.

In front of Walgreen's, Thane hailed a cab. He gave the driver his apartment address, nervously lighted a cigarette, and sat there on the edge of the leather upholstered seat, staring unseeingly out the window during the journey.

The apartment in which Thane lived was a four room affair in a towering building on North State Parkway. He had the driver drop him off half a block from the address—on a sudden change of mind —and, on leaving the cab, started down an alley which would take him around to the rear of the building.

He was able to gain entrance through the back freight door which was left open until three-thirty every morning for the convenience of those residents of the building who parked their cars in garages along the alley.

He didn't have to pass the night clerk at the switchboard, this way, and the night porter was—as Thane had known he would be— conveniently asleep.

* * * *

Thane used the freight elevator to reach the fifth floor where he and Lynn had their apartment.

There were a dozen apartments similar in size and floor plan on the fifth, and Thane's was at the end of the corridor, facing the street front and the lake considerably beyond.

Thane encountered no one going through the corridor. He was able to let himself into the apartment without being seen.

The place was in darkness, and Thane closed the door softly behind him and waited, holding his breath and listening for full half a minute before he reached for the light-switch that illuminated the small front hallway of the apartment.

Thane blinked in the light and waited for another half minute with his hand on the switch. Then he went into the living room.

The light from the hallway streamed past Thane into the living-room, giving it a gray, ghostly visibility. His eyes moved slowly across it, from the windows to the bookcases to the right of them, the easy chair, phonograph-radio, davenport, tables, desk, other chairs, the lamp—until suddenly the sight of these familiar things blurred in the mist that came to his eyes. They were the first tangible evidences of the sane, normal, happy life that had been his but hours before. They were, each of them in its small way, integral pieces of a life that was suddenly shattered in an explosive horror of blood and terror and murder.

Thane stepped across the room and turned on the lamp behind the easy chair. Then he saw the book, lying face downward to keep the place in it, beside the chair.

A book Lynn had been reading.

He looked at the ashtray on the low table beside the chair. It was heaped with cigarette butts, the ends of which were stained with Lynn's lipstick.

Thane turned away, went into the dining room, past the buffet, past the small cocktail bar, pushed through a door into the kitchen. He snapped on the kitchen light.

On the sink stood a cocktail shaker with a silver bar spoon in it. Thane went over to it. It was only three quarters full, and the Martini in it was warm, stale. A single cocktail glass stood beside the shaker. It was sticky, and there was half a Martini still in it.

He remembered Lynn's voice on the telephone that afternoon.

"I'll stir up a nice tall shaker of Martinis," she had said.

Thane turned off the kitchen light and went back into the living room. He stood there a moment, looking around uncertainly, until his eyes stopped at the desk in the corner, and he knew what he had subconsciously been seeking.

Perhaps Lynn had left a note.

Almost always, even when angry, Lynn would leave a note if she went out somewhere.

Thane could see from where he stood, however, that there was no note on the desk.

Mechanically, not aware that he was doing so, Thane found his cigarettes and lighted a smoke.

He stood there motionless a minute more, then turned and started for the bedroom off the hallway.

He didn't turn on the overhead light as he entered the bedroom; he reached for the cord of one of the lamps on Lynn's dressing table.

The scent of Lynn's perfumes made him swallow hard against the sudden lump in his throat. He looked around the bedroom.

The bed had not been slept in.

Lynn's red mules lay in a corner by her boudoir chair, a housecoat was thrown carelessly across the back of the same chair. Thane's eyes went to the night table beside the bed. There might be a message on the pad beside the telephone.

There wasn't.

He thought to look in the closet then—and found what he was dreading.

Lynn's overnight case was gone.

SO, he realized an instant later on looking through her dresses, were five or six of her favorite gowns. Thane stepped over to her dresser and opened the drawers methodically. Her lingerie, so carefully folded and neatly arranged as it generally was, was disordered and much of it gone. So were her stockings, handkerchiefs.

Thane closed the last drawer and stepped over to Lynn's boudoir table. He opened the jewelry case atop it, saw that some of her clips, rings, and necklaces were gone.

He took off his hat, then, tossing it wearily, carelessly, onto the bed. He walked over to the bed and sat down, head in hands. Minutes passed, and he noticed his cigarette long enough to straighten up and crush it out in an ash tray on the night-table.

Again, he put his head in his hands and closed his eyes wearily against the ache and the nausea and the horror that swirled fog-like around his mind.

He didn't know what he was going to do. He didn't know where he was going to go. He was too sick, too tired, really to care.

In the silence Thane was able to hear the ticking of the clock on the mantel above the living room fireplace. Against the raw, red abrasions of his mind the ticking was a cruelly malignant physical force—like water dropping rhythmically, ceaselessly on the forehead.

Thane put his hands against his ears and the sound of the ticking stopped, but the rhythm continued achingly in his head.

He rose, reaching for his hat behind him, and as he turned around he saw the glitter of the gun.

It was on the floor in a corner of the closet, shining dully, evilly, mockingly.

Slowly, as if hypnotized by the beckoning glitter of the weapon, Thane crossed to the closet and picked it up, holding it in his hand, staring at it in stunned horror.

It was the same gun he had left behind him in the apartment of the murdered man; the same gun he had found in his hand when he'd regained consciousness a few hours before!

Thane placed the gun atop his own dresser, and turned back to the closet. He dropped to his hands and knees and began a swift, frantic search of the closet floor. Then he rose, and began to go through the pockets of his clothing on the closet hangers.

He stepped back from the closet, face drained of any emotion, eyes curiously hard. Then he turned, left the bedroom, crossing the hall to the bathroom.

Thane went through the linen hamper swiftly, and found what he was seeking at the bottom.

He brought it forth—a roll of towels—and removed the clean towel covering the roll. The towels beneath were stained with blood.

Thane frowned momentarily, and then recalled where he had left this roll of bloodstained towels. He had left it beside the telephone in the hallway of the apartment where the murdered man lay.

HE PUT the clean towel back around the bloodstained ones, rolled them all up again, and carried them with him back to the bedroom.

Thane put the roll on the dresser, beside the gun, and picked up the weapon.

He removed the magazine clip from the gun, breaking the remaining bullets out into his hand. Two shots had been fired from the weapon.

Undoubtedly the same shots that had slain the man he'd left back in the strange apartment. Thane put the magazine clip back in the automatic, then dropped the gun into his pocket.

He stepped through the door and went back into the living-room. He rummaged through the drawers of his desk there, not finding what he sought. He frowned for an instant, then on impulse went back to the dresser in the bedroom.

In the handkerchief box atop his dresser he found the cartridges for the gun. A box of them, full save for the bullets in the gun and the two that had been fired from it.

Thane wondered what else had been planted in his apartment. He reached into his pocket for his cigarettes, brought out an empty pack and tossed it to the floor. He found an unbroken pack of Lynn's brand—Luckies—on the cocktail table. He opened this, tapped out a cigarette, lighted it, and sat down on the davenport.

The change hadn't come over Thane consciously. It hadn't been as sharply defined as stepping from darkness into light. But it had occurred, he realized, when his eyes had first encountered the gun on the floor of the closet.

Yes, the sight of that weapon had done it. With whip-like suddenness it had brought him around—much like a sudden, stinging slap will bring a person back from wild hysteria to sanity.

As Thane's eyes had encountered that gun he hadn't had to reason. It was all there before his mind with crystal clarity. And in that split-second the symbolism and grim significance of the weapon's presence had served as the stinging slap which drove away his terror, his sick bewilderment.

In less time than it would take to deliver an actual physical blow, that gun on the closet floor had brought to Thane the flaming fury of a man beaten, frightened, mercilessly mauled, and suddenly unable and unwilling to stand any more of it. The rage that had flooded him on seeing the symbol of what was being done to him had been swift, cold—an icy torrent of hatred frozen by grim determination.

Fear and sickness had drained from him in that instant. And the sharp frigidity of unimpassioned rage had taken control. The presence of that gun had explained the absence of Lynn. They had taken Lynn—there was no doubt of it in Thane's mind as he saw that weapon on the closet floor.

And in touching Lynn they had snapped something in the soul of Richard Thane—had transformed him from a beaten, cringing quarry into an adversary whose veins held the chill savagery of crimson hatred.

Thane was aware of this newborn determination, and of the sudden clarity of purpose and reason which had come to him in the swift transition. He found himself realizing that he was utterly alien to the Richard Thane who had entered this apartment but minutes before.

He felt the torrent of hatred coursing through him, and understood that, somehow, it was a hatred beyond anything his emotions had ever experienced. A hatred that washed its crimson flood through his body yet cleaned and steeled his thinking. It was a drug, more than an emotion. It gave him strength and courage and washed away sickness and fear.

Thane looked at his hands. They were calm, strong—taut, perhaps, with the rage that steeled them—but utterly unshaken.

He rose from the davenport, crushed out the cigarette, put the package of Luckies into his pocket. Then he went into the bedroom. He picked up the cartridge box from the handkerchief box and dropped it into his pocket beside the gun there.

26

Picking up the roll of towels, Thane carried it back through the living room, the dining room, and into the kitchen. He dropped it down the incinerator.

The telephone began to ring as he was going back through the dining room.

His features registered no emotion. His stride neither faltered nor quickened as he went to the hall to answer.

CHAPTER IV

Thane picked up the receiver and stood there with it to his ear. He didn't say anything.

The silence was electric. Then a voice on the other end of the wire said:

"Who is this?"

It was a man's voice, although it was tenor, bordering on the feminine. Thane wondered, for the flicker of an instant, if it was a crude imitation of a woman's voice. Then he decided not.

"Who is this?" the voice repeated again. There was no change in its intonations, confirming Thane's decision that it was not an attempt at impersonation.

"This is Richard Thane," he said after a moment. "Who in the hell am I talking to?"

"That is not important," the high tenor voice answered. "What is important is that I can help you. You are in serious trouble, Thane. You would be wise not to refuse assistance."

Thane said nothing to this, although the speaker had paused, as if expecting Thane to say something.

"Do you understand me, Thane?" asked the voice.

"I'm listening to you," Thane said.

"You had better," declared the voice. "If you are willing to follow instructions, you might be saved from the electric chair. Look in your pocket for your card case, Thane."

The voice paused, and Thane reached into his inner suitcoat pocket. His card case, which he invariably carried there, was gone.

"The case is in the apartment of the man you murdered," the voice resumed.

Thane broke in. "Why didn't you bring it along to my apartment as long as you remembered the gun and the towels?"

"It seemed reasonable to leave the disposal of those items to you, Thane," said the voice. "As soon as you begin to attempt such a disposal you will undoubtedly realize how difficult they are to get rid of. And, of course, it seemed reasonable to give you some concrete evidence of the fact that arrangements could be made to save you from execution."

"I interpreted the gesture in that light," Thane said coldly. "All right. I understand the spot I'm in. Get on with it."

"It has been decided that only by your leaving town for a few days would it be possible to eliminate the circumstances which make your position so difficult at present."

"You mean, of course; go into hiding," Thane said.

"Not exactly," said the voice. "You wouldn't be hiding, unless the police were to connect you with the crime. If you were to leave town as I suggest, and under the circumstances I state, it might be possible to erase your connection with the murder completely."

"What do you mean by the circumstances you state?"

"Circumstances such as your time of departure, your destination, and so forth," the voice said.

"I'm to agree to those circumstances such as you suggest?"

"Really, Thane, it seems hardly likely that you are in a position to disagree with anything I might suggest. Incidentally, you must realize that you have been followed ever since you left the apartment of the man you murdered."

Thane's silence was an exclamation.

"Don't let it make you jittery," the voice resumed. "It was not by the police, of course."

Thane's lips were taut as he said:

"We were discussing the trip planned for me."

"So we were," the voice agreed imperturbably. "You have undoubtedly noticed the excess of currency in your wallet. You are to use it for transportation expenses, some thirty-five dollars of it, that is. The rest is sort of a preliminary bonus. It was placed in your wallet to make you aware of another fact."

"And what was that?"

"Simply that, in addition to being willing to help you clear yourself of the murder, it can be arranged for you to find financial assistance in an almost unlimited measure."

"And what conditions go with additional cash donations?" Thane asked.

"A certain number of specific conditions. But they are of no importance now. They can be discussed later, in a more leisurely fashion. Let us get back to your train schedule."

"Train schedule?"

"You are to leave from the Northwestern depot, tonight—or, I should say, this morning—at five o'clock. That is less than three hours from now, so please get your instructions straight. You will go to the depot at twenty minutes to five. You will purchase a round trip ticket to Woodburn. From ten minutes to five until five o'clock, you will be seated on a waiting bench at the east end of the depot, near the soda fountain. At five, go to your coach on the train—it leaves at six minutes after the hour. Do you have that straight?"

In a tight, steady voice Thane repeated the instructions to that point.

"Good. Your train will arrive at Woodburn—it's in Wisconsin, in case I forgot to tell you—at four o'clock in the afternoon. Take a room at the Woodburn Hotel—it's the only one in town—and stay in your room until further instructions are given you."

"How will they be given?"

"That is incidental," the voice declared. "You will follow those instructions when they arrive—that's all that matters now. Is everything quite clear?"

"Yes," said Thane. "What about my wife?"

"She is alive," the voice said casually.

"She had better be," Thane answered tonelessly.

The click on the other end of the wire told him the conversation was ended. Slowly, Thane put the telephone back in the cradle. He walked back into the living room, removed his overcoat, tossed it on the davenport.

He found the package of Luckies in the coat on the couch, took one, put the pack into his suitcoat pocket, and lighted his smoke with the silver Ronson on the cocktail table.

Thane glanced at his watch. It was twenty minutes to three. He sat there smoking, his eyes half closed, his expression a stolid mask of rage.

After a moment he loosened his collar and removed his tie. He stood up, shrugging out of his suitcoat, then his best. He walked into the bathroom, still smoking, and began to remove his shirt....

* * * *

When Thane stepped out of the icily stinging shower, he dried himself vigorously with a vast turkish towel, wrapped it around his waist, and opened the medicine cabinet.

He snapped on the tube lighting fixture above the mirror a moment later and went to work cauterizing the wound in his scalp with alcohol and iodine. He found some tape and gauze bandaging and cut them to fit the wound. Then he combed his hair carefully.

When Thane finished shaving he went into the bedroom where he found a fresh change of linen and selected another suit. He lighted another cigarette as he finished dressing.

In the kitchen, a few minutes later, Thane broke the seal on a bottle of MacNiesh he'd taken from the small cocktail bar in the dining-room. He got ice from the refrigerator and a glass from the cupboard over the sink and turned on the cold water faucet.

Holding the glass up to the light, Thane dropped an ice cube in it and drowned the cube under half a glass of Scotch. He held the glass under the water spigot and let it fill to the top.

Then he went back to the living room and walked over to the window, glass in hand. He parted the curtains and peered down into the street five floors below.

A car was parked directly across the street from the apartment building and several more were parked on the west side of the street, but three or four buildings down. In one of those cars, Thane felt certain, was the person or persons who had followed him from the scene of the murder until he at last returned here.

Thane could see no one on the sidewalks, though it would be possible, he realized, for the building to be watched from the shadow of any doorway within range.

He let the curtain drop back in place and went over to the davenport and sat down.

His watch showed that it was a quarter after four, and abruptly Thane finished his drink and stood up. He crushed out his cigarette on the glass top of the cocktail table and picked up his polo coat from the couch.

When he had donned his hat and coat, Thane took the automatic from his pocket, removed the magazine clip, emptied the cartridges from it, and dropped them under the cushions of the davenport. Then he brought forth the cartridge box, reloaded the gun completely, snapped the clip back into the weapon, and put the box of cartridges and the gun back in his pocket.

Before he left the living room he paused a moment, looked around, then walked into the hallway. When Thane closed the door of his apartment behind him all the lights were burning as he had left them.

Thane took the regular self-operation passenger elevator down to the lobby.

As he passed the switchboard and desk, the bespectacled, pallid, thin-faced young divinity student who served as night clerk looked up from a theological text and nodded.

"Up early, Mr. Thane," he observed, eyes and expression curious.

"Or out late," Thane answered. He pushed through the double doors and stepped out into the street. The rain had stopped again, and the streets were fresh, black and damp under the lights.

Thane stopped at the sidewalk deliberately, fishing for a smoke as he stared at the car parked directly across the street. By the time he had lighted his cigarette he was certain that there was no one in the car.

He turned right, then, and walked the block and a half down to Division without pausing to look back over his shoulder. As he had known there would be, several cabs were parked in front of an all night sandwich shop on the corner of Division and State.

Thane crossed the street and climbed into the first of these cabs. A moment later the driver—who had been talking to the cabbie in the taxi behind his own—came around, hopped in behind the wheel, and said:

"Where to?"

"The Northwestern depot."

The driver was talkative at first, and somewhat insistent on giving Thane the inside track on allied military strategy as he saw it, but after a few blocks with only automatic grunts for reply, he lapsed into silence.

They went over to La Salle, then south across the bridge, and west again, following Wacker Drive to the turn that took them up to the east entrance of the depot.

Thane got out and gave the driver a dollar bill and a quarter. A tired redcap slouched forward, saw Thane had no luggage, and went back to his argument with an equally tired baggage-man.

Thane pushed through the doors and into the depot.

Save for a group of some seventy soldiers in a far corner of the waiting room, the vast first floor of the depot was virtually deserted. Thane went over to the ticket wickets and purchased a round trip to Woodburn, Wisconsin.

"Train leaves at five-oh-six," said the man behind the grille.

Thane nodded, put the envelope with his ticket inside his pocket, and walked over to the steps leading to the second floor past the train gate section.

The depot clock on the south wall of the second floor read eleven minutes to five. Thane turned left and walked down to the sector of waiting benches at the extreme east end of the room.

He passed a group of men in overalls, obviously farming people; several synthetic blondes overly dressed and overly painted who stared openly at him, snapping their gum as they chewed it; a sailor stretched full length on a bench, head on his ditty bag, sleeping; and a fat Mexican woman who stared dully at a brown-skinned child wrapped in blankets on her lap.

He wondered vaguely which of them were waiting for the same train as he.

He took a seat on a deserted bench facing the corridor which joined the smoke-stained old depot with the ultramodern Daily News Plaza building, picked up a copy of the Herald American which had been left there, and pretended to read the headlines.

Thane wondered if one of the four people sitting with their backs to him at the soda fountain just to the left of the corridor was the person assigned to check on his obedience to instructions.

Over the top of the paper he tried to decide this by staring intently at their backs.

He realized that, from their vantage points on the stool before the counter, any one of them, by means of the long mirror behind the counter, could watch him intently without revealing identity.

* * * *

One of the persons on the stools—they were all men—rose, paid his check, and turned around, starting in Thane's direction. He was a short, stumpy man with a ponderous paunch. He wore a dark blue overcoat with a chesterfield collar, and a Homburg sat jauntily on one side of his fat head.

Thane lowered his paper and stared openly as the fat man approached him.

The fat man, seemingly unaware of Thane's appraisal, busily picked his teeth with his thumb nail, regarding the nail disappointedly each time he removed it from his mouth. He was still engaged in this absorbing occupation as he waddled past Thane.

Thane relaxed after, following him with his eyes, he saw the fat man start down the steps in the center of the depot toward the first floor.

Thane put aside the paper and the pretense of reading it. He lighted a cigarette and continued to stare at the three men who remained on the stools at the soda counter.

Behind him the Mexican woman's baby woke and began to cry. Thane looked at his watch as the woman's voice began to soothe the child in her foreign tongue.

It was four minutes until five o'clock.

The Mexican baby had been silenced by some swift magic, and the drone of the conversation of the farmers came to Thane's ears.

One of the three remaining at the counter climbed off his stool and paid his check. The cash register rang, and the man turned around, stretching elaborately.

He was medium-sized, thin, and wearing a black overcoat which revealed brass buttons on his suitcoat as it fell open. The man held a uniform cap in his right hand, and Thane identified him as a brakeman or conductor.

He paid no attention to Thane as he sauntered by.

Thane looked again at his watch. One minute to five. He dropped his cigarette to the marble floor, crushing it out with his toe. He stood up, looking casually around.

Certain though he was that he was being watched, Thane found it impossible to tell from where or by whom. The fountain in front of him had, by its location and the explicit instructions that he sit in proximity to it, seemed like the most logical vantage point for his watcher.

Thane stared for a moment at the two men who remained at the counter. One of them was engaged in conversation with the night attendant who was changing the coffee cisterns. The other was reading a paper. It was impossible to tell if either of them was the man assigned to watch him.

Thane turned away and started toward the staircase in the center of the room. Ten or twelve yards on, he stopped and turned.

The man who had been reading the newspaper had climbed off his stool and was opening his overcoat to get to his wallet. His back was still to Thane.

Thane was fully a hundred and fifty feet from the counter, but when the man turned to face him, there was something in the faintly distinguishable lines of his features and his general physical appearance that seemed vaguely familiar.

Thane sensed, rather than knew, that the fellow had seen him staring at him. At any rate, the man turned around—so casually as to be completely unsuspicious—and said a few words to the man who remained on the stool.

Frowning, Thane weighed the advisability of going back, of walking up to the counter and confronting the chap openly. Then he decided against it, turned away, and continued toward the staircase. The chances were a hundred to one in Thane's favor that the fellow would be on the train with him when it left the depot, he realized, and the tedious journey to Woodburn would give him plenty of opportunity to carry out whatever course of action he deemed best in regard to his watcher.

In the track gate section a gate-man was calling out an endless string of small Wisconsin towns.

"On traaaaak sevvvvun!" he concluded.

It was five o'clock.

Thane presented his ticket at the gate to Track Seven and was passed through. The Mexican woman with the baby was up ahead of him, a cord-bound, splitting suitcase under one arm and the baby under the other. She waddled frantically, as if the hissing steam of the engine far ahead indicated immediate departure.

Thane frowned as he walked along the line of coaches—the Woodburn car was far up in front—and tried desperately to recall what had struck him as familiar about the appearance of the man with the newspaper at the soda fountain.

He had seen him but briefly—and from a considerable distance, of course. But there had been something—something—Thane tried to recall what it was, then temporarily abandoned the effort. He walked on toward his coach.

Thane was staring out the window and the train was starting to move when the explanation for the familiarity of the man with the newspaper clicked into place.

Thane's features went rigid, then white, and his hand clutched convulsively at the arm of his chair. It was incredible—utterly impossible!

Nevertheless Thane was numbly convinced of it. The chap's size, girth; his amiable bland moon face below his hat brim; his round button nose with the aggressively outthrust jaw below!

The man with the newspaper was the same man Thane had talked to several hours ago at the Idle Moment Tavern; the same pleasantly informative bartender who had so innocently related what he had seen occur between Thane and the murdered man. The train was clearing the station, now, and gaining speed.

It was seven minutes after five...

CHAPTER V

The train to Woodburn moved as reluctantly toward that destination as a child on the way to school. The stops along the route were innumerable; the delays at some of the stops, minor eternities.

Thane had traveled the length of the train twice within the first half hour of the journey. His inspection had failed to reveal any sign of the moon-faced, amiable, yet paradoxically mysterious little bartender.

Had his state of mind held anything other than the cold, unshakable hatred that it did, Thane might well have written the incident in the depot off as optical imagining prompted by hysteria.

But he had captured that fleeting glimpse of the man with the newspaper. Captured and held it in his mind while it was still fresh, until it was at last an indelible sketch in his memory. A sketch he could view and analyze and view again so that there was no longer any doubt of what he had actually seen.

It was almost impossible to link the blond little man to the hideous recollection of his discovery of the body in the strange apartment.

And yet such a link was now established by cold fact.

Thane had been utterly certain, in his conversation with the barkeep, that the amiable, though stupid, little man had been telling nothing but the truth.

The presence of the barkeep in the station, of course, washed away the belief Thane had had in the fellow's story. More sinister than that, it introduced the barkeep as the first identifiable figure in the hideous conspiracy against Thane.

It was impossible, of course, to imagine what role the barkeep was playing in the drama. Thane suspected even though realizing that he might be still guilty of underestimating the moon-faced fellow, that the barkeep was working as an underling for keener and more malicious superiors.

And yet the chap had seemed so open-faced, honest, genuinely unconcerned in his conversation with Thane.

36

There was no possibility of relating either fact, Thane knew. And to accept one would be to discard others. Nevertheless, each fact stood solidly by itself and only when linked did either seem utterly, maddeningly more tangled.

Thane had ended his second inspection of the train cars in the smoking room, and it was there, burning cigarettes one from the other, that he tried to bring reason to the madness.

Eventually he turned his mind to other and less impossible facets of the enigma, trying to establish conclusions from factors which—if considerably more cloudy—were at least in the realm of more tangible conjecture.

He tried once to paint an imaginary picture—by using the most reasonable processes of elimination—of the manner in which he had been shanghaied after having been drugged in the tavern on Washington.

He doubted if a cab had been used. The chance of getting one immediately was not always certain, and such a delay might have proved risky to his abductor.

It occurred to Thane, then, that his stopping in at the little tavern, as he had done, had been purely by accident, an impulse of the moment.

The person who had slipped the drug into his drink could have had no way of knowing that he would stop in there, or that he would stop anywhere—for that matter—before going home.

Thane paused in his reflections to wonder what the barkeep's part in the conspiracy had been. He wondered, too, if the murdered man had actually been in the bar under the circumstances the bartender had related. Perhaps the barkeep had put the drug in his drink, perhaps not. But Thane was certain that the moon-faced fellow had been an accomplice, if not the perpetrator of the drugging.

But, at the moment, the question of who had drugged him was not as important as why he had been drugged and how his accidental entrance had fitted in so perfectly with the timing of the person who had accomplished the fact.

The pattern at that point of the enigma seemed to be based utterly on happenstance. Thane frowned, certain that this was not the case at all. The rest of the pattern was too coldly planned to be based on such a shaky beginning.

Some mind, or minds, had cunningly, maliciously planned a murder for a certain time on a certain night. The same mind or minds had also planned to find a stooge for the purpose of framing the murder on him within an hour or so of the actual time of the crime.

He, Richard Thane, had been selected for the frame-up, and the scheme had gone through without a hitch.

But why he?

Because of a momentary impulse which turned his steps into a small, apparently respectable tavern he had visited less than six times before in the past year? Because he had just blundered into the path of the person seeking a fall guy for a frame-up?

The supposition did not fit the other details surrounding the enigma, particularly the details based on the high, tenor voice which had spoken to Thane over the telephone.

Everything about that conversation had indicated that the police did not yet know, and would probably never know, about the murder of the gray-moustached man in the strange apartment. The threat held over Thane's head by the mysterious, almost effeminate voice on the phone, had been the disclosure to the police of the murder for which he had been so damningly framed.

Thane realized, from the import of the conversation, that the speaker had been almost certain it would not be necessary to use the threat of exposure to the police as anything more than just a threat. He had taken it for granted that Thane would comply to the demands made of him, rather than face a murder charge which had been made air-tight against him.

This, then, placed the emphasis more on the frame-up as a weapon, than as a cunning scheme to shove guilt into another's hands. Whoever had slain the man with the gray moustache had seemingly been brazenly certain of his ability to keep the crime from the eyes of the police. Thus, the only motivation for framing the crime on another would appear to be to secure a throttling grip of blackmail to be used with a purpose.

Thane frowned deeply again, some of the stolidity of his expression leaving briefly in the grim business of concentration.

For what purpose would anyone blackmail Richard Thane, a young, none too important, specialist in international legal contract matters?

Money was immediately eliminated. Thane had a comfortable income, but nothing that would appeal to a blackmailer. Too, the twenty-five hundred dollars that had been placed in his wallet led in the opposite direction from such a conclusion. Blackmailers seeking money don't stuff their victim's wallet with it.

That money in his wallet had been placed there to add to the forceful demands that would be pressed upon him. The safety of his wife had been the crowning point in the pressure. The murder and the threat of his going to the chair for it; the money, and the broad hint that there could be more of it; Lynn, and the unspoken threat against her life.

Those were the three cudgels of blackmail selected by his adversaries.

But for what could he be possibly blackmailed? Of what use could he be to anyone to the extent where murder, much money, and the brink-edge of additional murder meant nothing when balanced against that person's wishes?

The question was utterly unanswerable.

Thane's eyes were growing heavy-lidded, in spite of the restless, inquisitive clamor of his mind. Physically, the hours he had been through began to set his every nerve to a numb, aching weariness that would not be denied.

Thane rose from his seat in the smoker, flipped his cigarette accurately into a brass spittoon three feet away, and started back up the string of trains until he was again in his own coach.

The dim blue sidelights were on in the coach, and the blinds drawn. The other occupants of the chair-car were apparently sound asleep by now.

Thane slipped into his seat, grateful that it was occupied only by himself. He had removed his overcoat carelessly in his first hour on the train, and placed it in the iron holding elevation where, lumped, and blandly unsuspicious, it had passed without attention.

He took his coat down, now that he planned sleep of a sort, and spread it over his knees, blanket fashion, with his right hand inside the pocket, closed around the gun.

It was easier than Thane had thought it would be. His heavy eyelids closed wearily, while the clicking rhythm of the train faded farther and farther from his ears, and at last there was oblivion and rest...

* * * *

Thane awoke four hours later, tumbling from a chasm of blackness and wind into a world of stinging light. He opened his eyes, squinting into the morning sunlight pouring through the window by his chair.

The rolling fields and fences margining the farmlands they were passing held Thane's attention hypnotically for fully half a minute, until he remembered.

He sat up, glancing sharply at his watch.

A quarter after nine.

39

At a quarter after nine yesterday, Richard Thane had said good-bye to his wife, Lynn, at the door of their apartment on North State Parkway.

At nine-thirty yesterday, Thane had opened his office, taken off his hat and coat, and seated himself behind his desk to open his morning mail.

An ordinary morning in the life of an ordinary, moderately successful young lawyer.

And now Richard Thane was moving toward a rendezvous in an obscure Wisconsin town. A rendezvous already prefaced by death and blood and violence. A rendezvous which Thane had determined to end in further blood and considerably more violence, should he get the chance for vengeance.

Thane had no precise plans. But he had a gun, and a cold, overwhelming hatred.

Something could be accomplished with those twin weapons, provided he kept them carefully reined.

Thane suddenly became aware that his hand was still closed around the gun in the pocket of his polo coat. He sat up and removed the blanket-like position of the coat, being careful that the gun did not drop out as he put the garment casually over his arm.

He stood up and stretched his cramped muscles, yawning involuntarily. He picked up his hat, and with his coat over his right arm, started for the washroom at the front end of the car.

When Thane emerged from the washroom he was considerably freshened, having splashed icy water over his burning eyes, scrubbed his face thoroughly, and combed his hair.

He lighted a cigarette as he moved down the aisle, deciding to make another inspection of the cars on the train. Passing his chair he dropped his hat on the seat, but kept his coat casually draped over his arm.

Four cars from the smoker, Thane found the man he had been seeking.

The bartender was sitting in a car washroom, reading a newspaper and smoking a cigarette, when Thane walked in on him and knocked the paper from his hands to the floor.

"All right," Thane said quietly. "Start telling me the truth."

For a moment the moon-faced barkeep gaped stupidly, unbelievingly, at Thane. Then words tumbled hoarsely from his lips.

"I—I thought you was asleep...last time I looked... I thought that —"

"Skip all that," Thane ordered. He continued to keep his voice level, low, hard.

The barkeep looked wildly behind Thane toward the entrance to the washroom.

"You wouldn't want to start any commotion," Thane said. "It wouldn't be a healthful pastime. Even if someone happened to walk in here, you'd be smarter and considerably more alive, if you kept your mouth shut until they'd left."

"Okay," the barkeep gasped. "Okay. I won't do nothing foolish. I promise."

"You don't have to promise," Thane said. "All you have to do is begin explaining." Thane moved his coat from his arm as he spoke, put his right hand in the pocket where the gun was, then draped the garment over his arm again.

THE barkeep saw the outline of the weapon against the coat and went several shades paler.

"Sure," he said, and his voice was a strangled whisper. "Sure. I'll explain anything you wanta know. Anything. I'll admit I lied to you when you came into the place around two o'clock this morning."

"Who drugged my drink?" Thane demanded.

The barkeep cleared his throat, his blue eyes were watery. He gulped.

"I did," he said.

"Why?" Thane asked.

"A guy gave me ten bucks to—" he stopped at the look that came over Thane's face, gulped frantically, and bleated: "I'm telling it to you straight, honest-to-God, Thane!"

Thane looked at him impassively.

"It's your story," he said coldly. "And your hide that depends on it. How do you know my name?"

The last question seemed to catch the bartender off-balance. His eyes popped, he gulped, and finally found voice.

"F-f-from the dame," he said.

"Dame?" Thane's voice questioned coldly.

"Yeah, sure, the dame. The dame that came into the Idle Moment around ten o'clock last night. She said she was looking for you. She said you'd called her from the place, and I ast her when you'd called and what you looked like. She described you, and said you'd called earlier, a little before six o'clock."

Thane's face was hard.

"What did she look like?" he demanded.

The bartender relaxed a trifle at this indication that his story might be under consideration, but perspiration continued to wilt his collar and bead his bald head.

"She was a small, trim, blonde dame, with a kinda turned up nose, and a straight, pretty little mouth. She was worried. She was wearing a brown fur coat. She was a looker," the barkeep concluded.

"The dame you described is my wife," Thane said coldly. "Why do you pretend you don't know that?"

The bartender's eyes widened in surprise.

"How should I know that?" he demanded plaintively, bewilderedly. "How should I know that?"

Thane stared at him, then said:

"What did you tell her?"

"I told her what I told you when you came back. I told her you got sick all of a sudden, and that a guy who said he was a pal of yours helped you out. I said for all I knew you'd gone home to sleep it off. She ast me what time that was, and I told her. She left, then."

"What did you do after she left?" Thane asked.

The barkeep looked worriedly puzzled again. "What did I do? What did I do? Why, I went back to serving drinks to customers, of course, But I was beginning to worry a little for fear maybe the mickey the guy gave me ten bucks to put in your drink had been too strong. I began to worry for fear maybe the thing was gonna backfire trouble on me."

"What do you mean, trouble?"

"My job, of course," said the barkeep. "My job and maybe thirty days in the Bridewell for getting mixed up in something that wasn't too ripe."

"Tell me about the stuff you put in my drink. Tell me exactly how it happened."

The bartender, face shining with sweat, cleared his throat again.

"Sure," he said hoarsely, "sure!" He gulped. "And this'll be the straight stuff, so help me God. I'll tell you just how it happened."

"That would be wise," said Thane.

"You hadn't come into the place yet, when this customer comes in and—"

"What customer?" Thane cut in.

"I don't know his name," the barkeep said. "He was a regular customer for the past couple months. A big guy, about six feet two and two hundred and twenty. Not fat. Not old. Maybe forty. Always dressed good in expensive clothes."

42

The barkeep had been looking at Thane as if he'd expected some sign of recognition in his listener's face.

"You don't know him?" the barkeep asked.

"No," said Thane.

"He generally came in with the guy I described to you as the one who took you out of the place," the barkeep offered.

Thane frowned. "You mean the man with the gray hair, gray moustache? The man you told me took me out of there?"

The barkeep nodded eagerly. "Yeah. That's right. You know him, so I figured you'd know this friend of his I was talking about—the big fella. They generally came into the place together, like I was saying."

"Go on with the story," Thane said.

"Well, this big guy, the friend of the guy with the gray moustache —like I said—came into the place before you did. He was alone and the guy with the gray moustache wasn't there waiting for him like he sometimes did. This big guy takes a seat at the far end of the bar and beckons me over. I smile and say hello and ask him what he'll have, or would he rather wait until his friend—meaning the guy with the gray moustache—got there. You see, they always drank to- gether, and I figgered maybe he'd wanta wait for his—"

"Yes," said Thane impatiently. "I understand. Get on with it."

"Well, this big guy says he's gonna pull a stunt on his friend with the gray moustache and he wants me to help. I laughs and makes a joke like, 'sure, anything short of murder,' and the big guy laughs and says he'll see to it that his friend never knows I helped in the joke on him, so I needn't worry about that. Then he takes out his wallet, pulls out a ten spot and tosses it on the bar. My eyes pop, of course, since that ain't peanuts for a tip. The big fella pulls the pack- age out of his wallet, then, and tosses that on the bar beside the ten bucks. It's a little paper package about an inch square. White. I ask him what is it, a mickey? He laughs and says it's like a mickey, ex- cept that it don't cause as much trouble as a mickey and don't send a guy running to the washroom all night. He says it's a harmless bromide, or something like that, and nothing to worry about."

The barkeep paused for breath, then went on.

"Of course I know what the big guy means, all right, but I ask him does he want me to put that mickey in one of his friend's drinks? He asks me what in the hell do I think he means. I take a second squint at the ten bucks, and say I don't know if I oughtta do anything like that. It might get me in trouble, I say. The guy picks up the ten bucks and reaches for his wallet to put it away. Am I ass enough to think that there was something wrong with it, he asks nasty-like. It's just an idea he had for a joke, and if I don't wanta pitch in, okay, he says. I can't stand the sight of that ten bucks going out the window, so I tell him, okay, okay, I'll do it if he promises not to tell his friend I'm the one who gave him the mickey. I say, after all, I don't wanta get in trouble with no one."

"Then the big fellow left?" Thane asked.

The barkeep nodded. "Yeah. He gave me the ten bucks and the paper package with the powder in it. He told me his friend with the moustache would be in in a little while, and not to let on that he— the big guy—was there. I asked the big guy if he wasn't gonna come back, and he said sure he was. He said he'd be back about ten minutes after his friend came in. I ast him how he'd know when his friend came in, and he said he'd know, all right, since he told his friend he'd meet him in the tavern at twenty-five minutes after five. Then he told me not to forget, and laughed, and went out."

"What time was that?" Thane asked.

The bartender frowned. "That was maybe two or three minutes after five," he answered.

"All right," Thane said. "Go on with the story."

The barkeep wiped the sweat from his bald head with a handker-chief, and cleared his throat nervously again.

"Well, I pocketed the ten bucks, and put the powder paper in the pocket of my shirt. Some customers came in, then, and I mixed their drinks. Then a couple more customers come in and I waited on them. It was a little after five-fifteen, by that time, and you come walking in. I fixed your drink for you, gave you the slug and told you where the telephone was. You had just gone into the telephone booth when the guy with the gray moustache comes through the door. He goes down to the end of the bar, a couple stools from where you've left your drink and sits down. I takes the powder pa-per from my shirt pocket, palms it, and walks over and asks him how he is and what'll he have to drink. He says he'll have Scotch and soda, and glances at his watch and looks around the bar. Then he wants to know if his friend—the big fella—has been in. I told him no, and went down to the other end of the bar to mix his drink. He can't see me, and I break open the paper and pour the powder in it, stirring hard, so's it'll mix good. Then I take the kicked-up drink down to him and put it under his snoot."

The bartender paused to collect his thoughts and his breath, then went on.

44

"I didn't wanta stand there gawking at him. It'd make him suspicious. So I turn away, nonchalant like, and start very slow toward the other end of the bar, making sure not to look back at him or do anything else that'd give it away. When I get down to the end of the bar, a customer starts gabbing, and it gives me a good excuse to kill time till he's done with his drink. About that time I'm beginning to worry more and more about maybe I wasn't so smart."

The barkeep stopped again to mop his bald head.

"Maybe two, three minutes passes while I chewed the fat with the customer," he resumed. "And then I turned around to look, more worried now, and seen that the guy with the moustache wasn't there, but that you were back from the telephone booth. It wasn't until you started to get glassy-eyed and teetering back and forth on the stool that I realize what's happened."

There was fright and supplication for belief in the bartender's eyes, now. He swallowed hard, and finished:

"You had come back and taken the wrong stool—they was just a few feet apart—and finished off the Scotch and soda I'd fixed for the guy with the moustache!"

CHAPTER VI

As the frightened, sweat-streaked face of the bartender turned up whitely to meet Thane's stare, there was a look of pleading anxiety in his eyes.

"So help me God, that's the level truth! You believe me, doncha? You believe me—you gotta believe me!"

Thane's expression was impassive.

"I believed you the first time," he said flatly, "and it didn't get me anywhere."

"Doncha understand why I lied then?" the little man pleaded hoarsely. "My God! I couldn't do nothing but tell you what I did. I couldn't stand there and tell you, sure, I doped your drink. My God! It was alla accident, so help me. But I couldn't explain it. I hadda lie!"

"Perhaps," said Thane, "you'd better tell me the rest of it."

The barkeep put his arms on his knees and cradled his sweat-streaked face in his palms. He continued huskily, wearily, staring at the floor of the washroom as he spoke.

"The rest happened like I told you the first time. You was glassy-eyed and wobbly, and all of a sudden the guy with the gray moustache was standing beside your stool—he must'a been to the lavatory—and keeping you from falling off. I was scared to hell, and went down to that end of the bar. I couldn't think of anything to say. I was afraid to tip off the guy with the moustache as to what it was all 'bout. My God! I couldn't explain to the guy with the moustache that you'd been mickied by a drink I'd fixed for him! So I asked him what in the hell was wrong."

"What did he say?"

"This is the truth," the barkeep declared vehemently, "just like I told you first. It almost knocked me for a gool. The guy with the moustache says that you musta been sopping it up all day, and that every now and then it hit you like that. He said you'd be all right, though, and that he was a friend of yours and that he'd take care of you. That's when I said you didn't look like you'd had too much when you come in. And he said you never showed it much."

There was still no change in Thane's expression.

"And so the man with the gray moustache was the one who took me out of there?" he asked tonelessly.

The bartender lifted his head from his hands and nodded with desperate vigor.

"Honest to God—he was! I'm leveling with you, so help me. The guy said he was a friend of yours and took you out. My God! Imagine how I felt then. Imagine how I felt. He was a friend of yours, and I was the jerk who'd balled the whole thing up from every angle!"

"He didn't return, after taking me out?" Thane asked.

The barkeep shook his head vigorously. "No. He didn't come back at all. That's how I figured he'd taken you home."

"Did the big fellow, the one you described as the man who put you up to the gag, come back like he said he would?" Thane asked.

The bartender nodded. "Yeah. He came back, all right. About five-thirty. It couldn'ta been more'n five minutes after the guy with the moustache took you out of the place."

"You told him what happened?"

"My God! I had to!" the barkeep groaned. "I told him, all right, and got out the ten dollar bill he'd give me and shoved it across the bar at him."

"What did he say?" Thane asked.

bartender winced at the recollection, and sweat broke out anew on his bald head.

"I never seen a guy so mad. My God! He was white! He just stared at me like he was gonna cut my heart out, and his lips moved without saying words. But I could read his lips, and I never knew there was so many dirty names in the English langwidge. My God!"

"Then what did he do?" Thane demanded.

"Nothing," said the barkeep. "He stood there maybe a minute throwing the book at me with them dirty names and looking like he'd be glad to burn out my eyes with pokers. Then he turned around and left. He didn't even take the ten bucks I'd shoved back to him."

Thane said suddenly:

"What's your name?"

"Faber," said the bartender. "Pete Faber."

"All right, Faber," Thane said. "Your story holds together beautifully up until now. But it will have to fall apart when you try to tell me why you're on this train, and why you're going to Woodburn."

The bartender looked perplexed. "Didn't I tell you? I—say, what do you mean, going to Woodburn?"

"You didn't explain that part, Faber," Thane said. "And I have a hunch you know damned well what I mean by Woodburn." His voice was suddenly harder than before, and challenging.

Faber looked frightened again. "My God! That's right. I didn't tell you about that part. He came into the bar about twenty minutes after you was there. Must'a been about twelve o'clock."

"Who?" Thane demanded. "Who came into the bar?"

"This mugg," Faber said. "He was about five feet seven, with shoulders as wide as a house. He was a blond, real natty dresser. He hadda banged in nose, like an ex-pug. Tough looking hombre. But the funniest thing about him was his voice."

Thane's expression flickered surprise.

"His voice? How do you mean?"

"It was high, and thin, almost like a dame's voice," Faber said, shuddering. "It woulda been funny as hell, except for the fact that this guy didn't look like no comedian; he looked like a killer. My God! It was all over his face and staring outta his eyes, that killer look."

"Go on," said Thane.

"He came to the end of the bar and waves me over," Faber continued. "He didn't waste no words. His first question is have I got a wife and kids. I told him no. He says that's good, because then I won't have no trouble leaving quick. Then, before I can ask what he means by this, he says that it's been decided that a quick trip outa town for a couple of weeks would be healthy for me. He says that I'd be able to forget about mickies in a week or so, and that it would be okay to come back in ten days or more, as long as I come back without any memory."

"What did you say?" Thane demanded.

Faber blinked in surprise.

"What did I say? My God! What could I say? I said when did he want I should leave. He said starting then and there. Then he left. I waited maybe ten minutes, then took off my apron and told the boss I was sick and going home. My God! I was sick all right. I went right to my room and packed my duds. I called the depot and found out there was a Wisconsin train leaving five-oh-six."

"Why Wisconsin?" Thane asked.

"I gotta cousin and his wife and kids living on a farm outside of Rhinelander," Faber said. "Only relatives I got within a hundrit

48

miles of Chicago. I figgered that'd be a nice quiet place to stay while my memory cooled off like it was told to."

"You certain your destination is Rhinelander, not Woodburn?" Thane demanded.

Faber nodded violently, fumbling inside his coat with trembling hands. He found his ticket envelope and handed it to Thane.

Thane opened the envelope and saw a round trip ticket between Chicago and Rhinelander. He put the ticket back in the envelope, handed it to Faber.

"You saw me when you turned away from the soda fountain in the depot?" Thane asked.

Faber nodded.

"My God! Sure I saw you. It almost knocked my hat off. But what in the hell could I do about it? Far as I knew, you mighta stopped in the depot for a candy bar. I waited until you were outta sight. Then I got on the train. It wasn't until we were fifteen minutes outta the depot when I spotted you coming down the aisle of my coach. I didn't have any idea you was on the train until then. My God! I didn't know what gave. I ducked into the washroom, locked myself in. I didn't come out for an hour. Then I took a chance, went through the cars, and saw you asleep in one of the front coaches. I came back here, figuring I could keep outta your way until I reached Rhinelander."

Thane stared at the moon-faced Faber. His expression had relaxed slightly around the mouth, and he took his hand from the gun in the pocket of his polo coat, fished in the pocket of his suitcoat and found a cigarette.

Every part of the bartender's story dovetailed perfectly into the circumstances which explained his presence on the train. Thane found himself believing the tale exactly as Faber had told it. But he had one final test on which he decided to base his belief or disbelief of the moon-faced barkeep.

Thane put his cigarette in the corner of his mouth, found matches and lighted it. He took a deep, reflective draught, and when he exhaled he said casually:

"You might be interested in knowing that the man with the gray moustache was murdered last night."

Faber had been staring at Thane, pleading his innocence with his eyes and sweat-stained face. He had no time to plan a reaction to the casually spoken statement.

The horrified shock on the bartender's face told Thane what he had been seeking to confirm.

Faber had been telling the truth this time. He had known nothing of the murder...

* * * *

Thane left the moon-faced bartender and returned to his chair car. It was twenty minutes after ten, and the train was slowing down preparatory to a small station milk-stop.

He put his coat back atop the luggage rack over his chair, removed his hat from the seat where he had left it, and sat down, closing his eyes tiredly and mentally assembling the pieces of information he had gained, preliminary to a fresh start on the incredible jigsaw.

For every new facet uncovered by Faber's story, a previously accepted one was lost. The arrangement of the pieces—as loosely as he had placed them—had been knocked asunder by the information he now possessed. The sorting and reassembling that would be necessary in view of his new knowledge would undoubtedly be no less difficult than his first efforts had been. But the pattern which they would ultimately form would be somewhat more certain.

Thane took a deep draught from the last of his cigarette, dropped it to the floor, and crushed it out with his heel. He leaned back, steepling his fingers, and started to pattern the scant and bewildering facts at his command.

"Thane, I'd like to talk to you a minute."

He opened his eyes, saw Faber standing beside his chair. The moon-faced little bartender looked both worried and awkwardly uneasy.

"About what?" Thane asked. "Is there something you held out on me?"

"The washroom," Faber said, "ain't occupied right now. We could talk better there."

Thane grunted and rose. He followed the bartender to the head of the coach and stepped into the washroom behind him. As Faber had stated, they had privacy there.

"I haven't held out nothing on you, Thane," Faber said earnestly. "That ain't what I had on my mind."

"Then what is on your mind?"

"Look," Faber said awkwardly, his shining brow creased in a frown, "it's like this." He hesitated again, then blurted: "This thing has me down in more ways than one. I'm in a spot that ain't so comfortable, but you seem to be knee-deep in something worse than I gotta worry about. I'm the guy who shoved you into the soup.

Maybe I made things worse by not giving you the straight dope from the start. Maybe I even gummed things up more by holding out on the facts from your old—your wife. I'm not a mental heavyweight, but I can catch on to things if I get time and room enough."

Thane looked at him expressionlessly.

"All of which leads up to what?" he asked.

"If there's anything I can do to hel—" he began, then stopped, coloring at the expression that came suddenly to Thane's face.

"Well?" Thane asked.

"I know what you're thinking," Faber said miserably. "I'm a mugg who'll take a ten spot to dope a drink. You figger I'd take half that amount to break an old lady's arm. Maybe I don't blame you. Anyway, I certainly took a runout in a hurry when that hood came into the bar and made faces and words at me. I pushed around plenty easy, and the more I've been thinking about it and wondering what color stripe I got on my hide, the sorer I been getting at myself. Maybe you won't believe it, Thane, but I was a tough nut twenty years ago. Nobody pushed me around anyplace, and that includes the prize ring. I—hell, I—ah—My God! Isn't there something I can do for you?"

Thane's expression was impassive once more. But his eyes were speculative.

"I don't think you realize how far you're sticking your chin out, Faber," Thane said, watching him.

"You're going to Woodburn," Faber said doggedly. "The conductor'll change my ticket."

"The man with the gray moustache didn't look pretty, dead."

"Could I look prettier alive?" Faber retorted.

"For all you know I could be a murderer," Thane said.

Faber shook his head positively. "Unh-unh. Not you. Guys like you don't get nasty that way."

Thane rubbed his jaw reflectively. He stared at the barkeep another moment. Then he said:

"You could recognize the man who gave you the ten dollars?"

"At a hundrit yards," Faber answered emphatically.

"And the blond yegg with the voice like a woman?"

"Hell, I could smell him from that distance," said Faber.

"All right," Thane said briefly. "It's your hide, not mine."

Faber pulled the gun more swiftly than Thane could blink. It had been a lightning grab that had whipped the automatic from a shoulder holster.

Thane's face froze as Faber held the gun unswervingly trained on his heart. Then the bartender laughed, and lowered the weapon.

"I brought this along for the farm stay," Faber said. "I didn't know but what maybe I'd need it. That blond with the dame's voice wasn't funny."

The moon-faced little bartender put the automatic back in the shoulder holster beneath his suitcoat. He grinned apologetically at Thane.

"I guess I wasn't brung up right," he said. "I could never make up my mind to ditch the rod, even after I'd been outa the rackets fifteen years."

A faint smile touched the immobility of Thane's expression. He looked at the bartender with a new respect.

"You'll do," he said.

Faber rubbed his bald head sheepishly.

"I was packing the rod alla time you was grilling me," he admitted. "You should never be so dumb as to hold a rod so clumsy-like in a coat, the way you did."

"What in the hell made you sweat so?" Thane asked.

"My God!" Faber replied. "I was thinking maybe I'd have to plug you, and what a hell of jam it would get me into." He sighed. "My God! I'm a yella so-and-so."

CHAPTER VII

It was ten minutes after four when Thane's train arrived at the unpretentious little station at Woodburn. While the engine bell clanged and the steam hissed, the local postmaster supervised the unloading of the mail bags onto a small baggage cart.

Thane descended the steps from his car to the station platform almost simultaneously with the cry:

"Boooooaarrrd!"

Thane looked around the station appraisingly. It was typical enough for a town of Woodburn's size. Baggage carts, waiting benches, a waiting room inside. He could see some of the town stretching a few blocks deep on the other side of the station. A small business district, boasting a theater and one floor department store, plus the usual number of other enterprises.

To the right of the station was a residential district. Narrow streets, trees that were leafy arches in summer and gaunt brown skeletons now.

The sign on the station as the train had pulled in had told Thane that the population of Woodburn was several hundred over five thousand.

The driving rods of the big locomotive up forward began to churn and the train picked up motion laboriously, cars banging in couplings, as Thane crossed the station platform and stepped into the small waiting room.

He had to wait some five minutes while the postmaster, baggage master, station master, and telegraph operator—in the person of a tall, spare, wiry old man with white, bushy eyebrows—discharged his chores in the order of their importance.

When the old man entered the waiting room at last, he surveyed Thane quizzically.

"What kin I do fer you, sir?"

"Can I send a telegram from here?" Thane asked.

"Don't see why not."

The old man unlocked the door leading into his ticket cage, reappeared a moment later behind the window, pencil in hand and pad

53

before him.

"Well, sir, who to?" he asked.

"G. Winters," Thane said, "Blufftown, Wisconsin."

The old man jotted this down on the blank.

"From who?" he asked.

"J. Crandall," said Thane.

"How you spell that?"

Thane told him.

"Want it sent night letter, or now?"

"Now," said Thane.

The old man shoved a telegram sheet through the window.

"Write it," he said.

Thane picked up the pencil the old man had left atop the blank, thought a moment, then rapidly scribbled a message. He shoved the pad and pencil back through the window grille.

"Arrived on schedule. See you later as arranged. Crandall."

The old man read aloud. He looked up at Thane. "Got two more words coming," he pointed out.

"That's all right," Thane said. "How much is the message?"

"You want it sent to the station at Blufftown, that right?"

Thane said that was right.

The old man told him the charges, and Thane pushed a dollar bill through the window opening. The old man found change, shoved it back at Thane. Thane started to turn away.

"Come to work at the plant?" the old man asked.

"The plant?" Thane frowned.

"New war plant just outside of town," explained the old man. "They're looking for help over there. Most everyone in town is working there now, seems like."

"No," Thane said. "No. That isn't why I'm here."

"I wondered," said the old man with easy candor. "Ain't usual to get passengers coming off the four-oh-six on Sunday during this time of year."

"I suppose not," Thane agreed. "Which way is the Woodburn Hotel?"

"Right on Main," said the old man. "Go out the same door you came in, turn right, go down to the end of the station, you'll see it. Sign over the sidewalk."

Thane nodded.

"Thanks," he said.

* * * *

54

Thane found the Woodburn Hotel and saw a little bit more of the town enroute. There was, it seemed, a second business street comprised principally of taverns in surprising number, another movie theater—boarded up and not in operation, however—and a bank.

Registering at the desk in the lobby of the Woodburn, Thane was subjected to a moderate amount of curiosity on the part of a few guests and the employees.

Although he had no luggage, a nondescript bellboy-porter showed him up to the second floor where his room was located, gave him his key, and asked if there was anything he'd like. Thane gave him a five dollar bill and told him to bring back some glasses, ice, soda, and a bottle of Vat.

Thane closed the door behind the boy and began an inspection of his room. A big brass bed that looked as if it would be comfortable, an oak dresser with the inevitable Gideon atop it, two chairs, a moderately roomy closet, good light and excellent ventilation due to its corner location and two windows, and a washbowl in a corner were what the room boasted. It lacked a bath and toilet, and Thane suspected he could find both down the hall.

He removed his coat, transferring the automatic to the under side of the pillow on the bed, tossed his hat on a shelf in the closet, and shrugged out of his suitcoat.

Then he sat down on the bed and lighted a cigarette.

He was smoking and staring at the worn floor covering when the combination bellhop-porter knocked on the door. Thane raised his voice and told him to come in.

"I thought there'd be a phone in this room," Thane said, as the boy arranged the bottles, glasses and ice on the dresser.

The boy looked surprised, then triumphant.

"You didn't see it," he said, opening a bottom drawer in the dresser. Then Thane saw the wires that must have been protruding, and the boy held the telephone up proudly.

"Leave it on the dresser," Thane said. "I wouldn't want to play hide-and-seek with it during the middle of the night."

The boy put the phone atop the dresser. Then he gave Thane a dollar bill and some change. Thane gave him a half dollar, and he left.

Thane fixed himself a drink, pulled one of the chairs over beside the bed and—using it as a table—placed the glass on its seat. He took his place on the bed again, tasted the drink, and leaned back against the bedstead.

He wondered how long he was going to have to wait.

* * * *

It had occurred to Thane more than once that this might be nothing but a hoax cleverly designed to remove him from the city long enough for his adversaries to accomplish further designs against him. But he had discarded this idea for the dual reason that he was unable to do anything else than accept the situation as it stood, and that other factors argued against it.

It was reasonably clear to Thane now, that his being involved in the thing had started accidentally. It had been the mixup in drinks which had snowballed him into the murder and terror which followed. The moment he had raised the drugged glass to his lips, his part in the gruesome mystery was cast.

Lynn's visit to the tavern where he'd been drugged had puzzled him deeply for a while, until he remembered having mentioned where he was when he'd made that call to her.

Undoubtedly she had grown worried when he failed to show up at the apartment. She had recalled what he had said about stopping in at a place around the corner from his office on Washington, and gone in search of him.

What had happened to her after Faber told her his story and she'd left the place, Thane couldn't guess. Faber had told him Lynn had been in around ten o'clock. She might have gone back to the apartment, then.

There was the possibility that Lynn had been followed from the apartment to the Idle Moment. She might have been waylaid on leaving the tavern. But that discounted the fact that he had found her overnight bag and some of her clothes gone. It seemed reasonable to believe, then, that she had returned to their apartment.

What had happened there was additional speculation. Someone might have been waiting there when she returned. The only thing that was certain in that respect, was that Lynn wasn't in the apartment shortly after one, when Thane had made his first call.

The fact that she had packed her bag, taken some of her gowns, indicated that violence had not been involved in her abduction. Or it indicated that someone else had thrown some of her things into the overnight bag before taking her along.

Thane crushed out his cigarette on the side of a wastebasket. He got up and took his empty glass over to the dresser, fixed himself another drink. He went back to the bed and resumed his position, lighting another cigarette as soon as he was comfortable.

Thane wondered if Faber had received his telegram in Blufftown all right. He took a deep swallow of his drink and speculated about the little barkeep.

Perhaps Faber would lose his stomach for the bargain he'd made. Perhaps he'd take another train back to Rhinelander and the place where he'd originally intended to hole up. Somehow, Thane didn't think so.

Thane got up from the bed, glass in hand, and walked over to the window. He stared down at the street for several minutes, unseeingly. Then he turned away, gulping down the rest of his drink and going towards the dresser to refill his glass, when he paused, frowned, and picked up the telephone.

The voice of the desk clerk came through a moment later.

"This is Mr. Thane. I want you to ring me before sending anyone up here, understand?"

"Yes, sir. You're expecting someone?"

"I am," said Thane. "But don't call me until they've started up."

Thane hung up and mixed himself another drink. He walked back to the bed, put the glass on the chair beside it, and stretched out again.

He looked at his watch. It was ten minutes after five. It was getting definitely dark outside by now. His short sleep on the train hadn't helped much, and his eyelids were heavy again. Thane crushed out his cigarette before dozing off....

* * * *

When Thane woke the room was in darkness. A glance at the luminous dial on his watch showed him that it was seven-thirty. He rubbed his eyes and sat up, blinking.

And then he was aware that something had wakened him. Some sound.

In an instant he knew. The bulky figure in the darkness by the door said:

"Easy, Thane. Stay just as you are. You're covered."

Thane stared hard into the darkness, adjusting his sight to the deeper black of that figure by the door. Slowly, silently, he moved his hand behind him, fingers searching for the gun beneath his pillow.

"Get out of the bed," the voice commanded, "and put both paws in the air. Then stand there until I draw the shades and turn on the light."

Thane's hand found the gun, closed around it.

57

"You heard me, Thane," the voice said. The bulky figure in the darkness moved a little away from the door.

Thane knew that it would be a matter of no more than several seconds to whip the gun forth and fire. He knew that he could kill the figure in the darkness. But his hand released the gun, leaving it behind the pillow, and he stood up from the bed unarmed.

"Okay, put 'em in the air," the voice said.

Thane raised his hands above his head, and the bulky figure in the darkness stepped quickly over to first one window, then the other, drawing the shades on both.

The room was considerably darker now, but Thane could still follow the outline of the man in the darkness.

There was a click, and light flooded the room.

Thane blinked, and saw his intruder standing beneath the light cord which hung from the ceiling. The man was holding a gun, pointed at Thane, and smiling.

Thane's exclamation was involuntary.

His intruder was short, stumpy, with a tremendous paunch. He wore a dark blue overcoat with a chesterfield collar. A Homburg sat jauntily on one side of his fat head.

This was the first man Thane had seen leave the soda fountain in the depot—the same man who'd passed by him without even glancing up from his absorbed picking of his teeth!

"Hello, Thane," he said. "Remember me?" He made a gesture with his thumb, as though picking his teeth, then laughed. "Get your coat on. We're going places."

Wordlessly, Thane stepped over to the closet, taking his polo coat from the hanger. He tossed it on the bed, took his hat from the shelf, and did the same with that.

Then Thane crossed the room to the chair by the window on which he'd draped his suitcoat. He buttoned his collar and pulled up his tie as he did so.

AS Thane donned his suitcoat, the obese, stumpy intruder walked over to the bed and picked up the polo coat. He patted it several times around the pockets, looked at the bedcover, then dropped it back.

The fat man stepped over to the door, keeping his gun on Thane, and said impatiently:

"Speed it up."

Thane slipped into his suitcoat and stepped over to the bed. It wasn't difficult, as he leaned forward to pick up his hat and coat, to slide the automatic out from under the pillow and conceal it beneath the coat.

He was carrying the coat on his arm as he joined the stumpy fat man at the door.

"Okay," Thane said. "Let's get going."

The fat man kept his gun in his pocket as they passed through the lobby. But he kept his hand on the weapon and, undoubtedly, his finger on the trigger.

The desk clerk called after Thane, and the fat man paused while Thane turned.

"What shall I say if that call comes through, Mr. Thane?" the clerk asked amiably.

Thane stared at him a moment.

"Say hello," he said. He turned, and walked out of the lobby, the fat man beside him, half a pace behind.

On the street Thane paused. He faced the fat man.

"What next?" he asked.

The black sedan rolled up to the curb beside them, at that moment, and the stumpy fat man jerked a thumb at it.

"We ride," he said.

Thane saw the driver of the sedan, then. He was blonde, hard faced, wide-shouldered. His nose had the pushed-in mark of an ex-pug. He was the hood Faber had described. The one who'd told Faber to leave town. The one with the voice like a woman—the voice Thane had talked to on the telephone.

"You get in the back, with me," said the fat man. "You first."

Thane opened the rear door of the sedan and got in. The fat man followed him, taking his gun from his pocket as he did so. He wheezed as he sat down, turned slightly, gun held in his lap, and grinned at Thane.

"Get going, Harvard," the fat man told the driver.

CHAPTER VIII

They were through the little town and into the outskirts of it in less than eight minutes. There was little traffic save for an occasional truck and three or four passenger automobiles, even though they followed a state highway for another five minutes after leaving the town.

At a junction in the highway, they took a smaller, fairly well paved road, heavily bordered by thick woods. After five minutes on this road, the woods began to thin out, and three minutes later, in a vast, heavily rutted clearing, Thane saw the outlines of a large, recently constructed factory.

As the car sped on past it, Thane remembered what the old man at the station had said about the new war plant outside of town. The fat man, noticing Thane's interest in the countryside, laughed harshly.

"Get your eyes full, Thane," he said. Thane's fingers closed tightly around the gun beneath the coat on his lap, then relaxed. Not yet. There was still Lynn to think of. He had to remember that.

They turned off onto a narrow, bumpy clay road several minutes later, and the blond hoodlum at the wheel slowed their speed perceptibly. Several hundred yards on, the car stopped.

"Okay," said the fat man. "We get out here."

The wide-shouldered, pug-nosed blond behind the wheel climbed out first, leaving the headlights on. He came around the front of the car and stood beside the front right fender, waiting. He had a gun in his hand.

"All right, Thane. Get out," the fat man said.

Thane's skin crawled. He swallowed hard. Supposing he had miscalculated? Supposing it was to be here, right now, the moment he stepped out of the car?

He thought of Lynn and his jaw hardened. His hand closed around the gun beneath his coat, and he leaned forward, opening the door. He stepped out into the sticky bank of the clay road, his eyes on the blond killer ahead of him, the coat still covering the gun in his hand.

60

Nothing happened.

"You gonna block the door all night?" the fat man snapped behind him.

Thane moved forward, and the fat man wheezed out of the car.

"All right, Thane," the fat man said somewhat breathlessly, "you walk along behind Harvard. I'll be right behind you."

The blond ahead turned and started up the road.

The fat man said: "No Olympic dashes, Thane. You wouldn't get a yard away before it'd be all over."

Thane walked on, passing the front of the car, his hand hard on the grip of his automatic. Behind him, he heard the fat man wheezing.

* * * *

The clearing was twenty yards ahead, off the road, and the blond called Harvard waited there at the edge of it while Thane and the fat man caught up with him.

There was a low, rambling shack of the sort used by construction companies in the center of the clearing. Lights burned in four of its windows.

The blond spoke as Thane and the fat man reached him.

"It will be best to let Thane walk in front now, Runt," he said. Thane recognized the thin, high, almost feminine tenor and the careful enunciation. Harvard was undoubtedly the one he talked to over the telephone, and unmistakably the one who'd told Faber to leave town. The disparity between the man's speech and appearance was chilling.

"All right. In front of us, Thane," the fat man ordered.

Thane stepped out in front of the two, and in this order they crossed the clearing to the construction shack. The door of the central section of the shack opened when they were less than five yards from it, throwing a blocked patch of light against the darkness. A blocked patch against which was silhouetted the figure of a tall, solidly built man.

No one said a word, and the big man left the door and went back into the shack.

A moment later and Harvard's gun was in Thane's ribs, while the thin tenor command, "Up the steps slowly," was given.

Thane obeyed, climbing the steps slowly, and stepped into the shack with Harvard's gun still against his back. Blinking in the sudden glare of light, Thane surveyed the big man sitting behind the scarred desk in the corner.

61

He was roughly as Faber had described him. Heavy-set without being fat, shoulders powerful but sloping rather than square. His face gave Thane the impression of a bulldog.—It was ruddy, smooth shaven, wide mouthed, and unpleasant. His hair was black, and thinning visibly above his forehead. He had combed it, unsuccessfully, to conceal the growing baldness. He wore a tweed suit that was darkish brown, adding to the impression of his massiveness.

He said, "Come in, Thane."

Thane moved to the center of the room, and the pressure of Harvard's gun against his back was gone. He heard the door of the shack shut behind him. The fat man whom Harvard had called Runt spoke.

"Here's the guy with the tough skull, boss."

Thane said quietly, "Where is my wife?"

The man behind the desk grinned. His teeth were very white against his ruddy face.

"You've come to take her home, I suppose?"

"Where is she?" Thane repeated.

"Take the gentleman's things, Harvard," said the man behind the desk.

The crashing blow Thane received on the side of his head caught him utterly unprepared. A sickening explosion of light and sound burst in his brain as he fell forward to the floor. A shot roared deafeningly through the room, and something made a metallic sound on the floor.

Thane realized foggily that his gun was no longer in his hand, and that his mouth was filled with blood, and that someone was cursing harshly.

He tried to get to his knees, but his senses were swimming and his balance gone. He slipped forward and his face struck the floor. He didn't lose consciousness, though everything reeled in a chasm of blackness.

"Pick him up," somebody said.

Hands grabbed him by the collar of his coat and jerked him to his knees. Then his face was slapped stingingly again and again, until he staggered to his feet.

The hands were on his arms now, as he teetered unsteadily and tried to spit the blood from his swollen mouth. He realized that his eyes were closed, and he opened them. The light stabbed painfully, and Thane realized that only one eye was open. He couldn't open the other.

The room was beginning to come back into focus. He could see the massive man in tweeds behind the desk, and the blond called Harvard at his side, glaring at a white-faced, terror stricken Runt. The hands were no longer on his arms.

The terrible flow of obscenity was coming from Harvard, directed at Runt. The blond hoodlum's thin voice was almost shrill in his rage. Finally he stopped.

"You ought to be plugged for being dumb enough to let him bring a rod along, Runt," the massive man behind the desk declared. His voice was calm, unhurried. "Another minute and he'd have been pouring lead at all of us. You can thank God I knew no one would hold a coat the way he was holding his. Get the hell out of the room before I give in to the impulse to have Harvard burn you."

Runt's ponderous paunch was heaving mountainously with the deep, gasping breaths he drew. His face was utterly white, his eyes glazed with fear. He staggered over to a side door and left the room.

The massive man behind the desk looked up at Thane now, grinning again.

"Do you always bring presents when you're invited to the country?" he asked.

Thane swayed sickly, his hand to his swollen mouth, and spit blood. His eyes glared wildly at his captors.

"Get him a chair, Harvard," said the massive leader.

The blond killer brought a chair around and placed it behind Thane. Thane slumped into it weakly.

"Give him a cigarette," the big man ordered.

Harvard extended a package of cigarettes to Thane. He took one, put it between swollen lips. Harvard struck a match and lighted it for him.

"I don't think we've been properly introduced," the man behind the desk declared amiably. "My name is Colver, John H. Colver, of Colver and Thurston. You've met my partner, Thurston, remember? You spent last night in his apartment until your untimely departure around one o'clock."

"Go to hell!" Thane mumbled.

Harvard stepped forward and slapped Thane across the mouth. The blow caused no pain. Thane's face was already numb.

"All right, Harvard," Colver said sharply. "Save the sadism for later." His eyes went back to Thane. "Your skull was too tough for us last night, Thane. You weren't supposed to come out of the fog until three o'clock or better. The police would have been there by that time, and all this unpleasant additional labor would have been saved me."

"Where is my wife?" Thane said thickly.

"She's still alive, Thane," Colver said. "You'll see her very shortly. It's a shame to think you could have spared her this merely by remaining unconscious another two hours in Thurston's apartment."

"Why did you do it," Thane managed through swollen lips.

"Kill Thurston? Or frame it on you?" Colver asked. "Why, I don't see why an explanation isn't due you. After all, you haven't gotten anything at all for all your trouble. We've really had to push you around, Thane. I suppose it would be courteous to give you the satisfaction, at least, of knowing why." He paused.

"Well?" Thane asked.

"But that would be far too melodramatic, Thane," Colver grinned. "You can find out why in hell. You'll be there shortly, you know."

Colver reached into the drawer of the desk before him and brought out a .45 automatic. He put it on the desk and shut the drawer. He looked at Harvard.

"Tell Runt to go out to the garage and start the motor in the Ford going. Tell him not to connect the hose from the exhaust until we bring Thane and his wife out there."

Harvard stepped to the door through which Runt had made his trembling exit. Colver turned back to Thane.

"Carbon monoxide," he explained. "The Ford will be closed tightly while you and your wife are in it. As soon as you are dead, we air things out for several hours, then Harvard chauffeurs your bodies to the high turn on Willow Road."

Colver stared at Thane for a reaction to this. The big man's eyebrows raised.

"Don't you know the high turn on Willow Road? Ah, but of course you don't. You're a stranger here. I quite forgot. Willow Road is half a mile behind my plant—the war plant you passed on your way here. The road circles Lake Luna. It's a small lake, this Luna, but like so many Wisconsin lakes it is particularly deep in certain spots. Spots such as the one just below the high turn on Willow Road. The Ford, with you and your wife in the front seat, will make quite a splash dropping into Lake Luna. It's almost two hundred feet from the road edge down the cliff beside it."

Thane's voice was hoarse, pleading, thickened by his swollen lips.

"My God, keep her out of it! Let her go—for God's sake! She's done nothing! She's—"

Colver smiled, cutting Thane off.

"She'll die painlessly, beside you. I think that's rather touchingly romantic. I'd like to spare her, Thane. She's quite lovely. However, you are both much better off dead. You and your wife and the bartender will be dead by morning. The bartender, of course, is the blundering ass who permitted you to take the wrong drink. Runt saw him purchase a ticket to Rhinelander in the depot. Harvard will drive up there, find him, and complete the job as soon as you are out of the way." Colver smiled again. "You three are the only persons who know anything even remotely connected with poor Thurston's death."

Harvard came back into the room, then.

"You told him?" Colver asked.

Harvard smiled, his cold eyes glittering.

"Quite explicitly," he said in his high, feminine voice.

Colver sighed resignedly. "I suppose you pushed him around for his error in not frisking Thane at the hotel."

Harvard was still smiling. He wet his lips.

"I'm not through with that fool yet," he said. Then he added, "I sent him out to the road to turn off the headlights on the sedan, first."

Colver nodded. "Good. Now I think we'd better get Thane's wife. He'll be happy to—"

The crash of the door banging open was like a pistol shot. Thane, Colver, and the blond sadist turned to gape at the doorway simultaneously.

Runt stood there, his face a twisted pattern of hysterical terror, his arms limp at his sides, knees shaking. And then Thane saw the hand poked out from behind the stumpy fat man—the hand holding an automatic.

"Hold it just as it is, boys!" a voice commanded. It was Faber's voice.

"For God sakes don't shoot!" Runt whimpered. Saliva drooled from the corners of his fat mouth.

"You move an inch, and I'll plug this guy. I gotta 'nother gun in his spine!" Faber's voice commanded.

Thane was out of his chair and on his feet. Harvard's hand was grabbing for the shoulder holster under his coat. Colver was the only one within quick reach of a weapon. He whipped up the .45 from his desk.

"You shoot," the voice of the barkeep, Faber, yelled, "and this yegg of yours get it!"

Colver snarled, "That's fine!"

Thane hurled himself in a savage rolling block at Harvard's legs at the same instant Colver's .45 roared.

As Thane crashed to the floor with Harvard, Runt's shrill scream blended in the echo of the gun blast. The scream choked off in an obscene, strangled curse ending in Colver's name, and Thane heard Runt's fat body smash to the floor.

Then there were other shots roaring almost simultaneously; and Thane found his hands locked tightly around the automatic Harvard had managed to drag from his shoulder holster. The blond killer was writhing frantically in an effort to roll out from under Thane's weight, and Thane ground his teeth until his jaw ached, forcing the sadist gunman's arm back farther and farther until there was the snap of breaking bone.

Harvard's scream rang horribly in Thane's ear. In the split second in which the blond gunman went inert, Thane grabbed the gun from the floor where it had fallen.

As Thane tried to climb free of Harvard, the gunman's frantic grab with his good arm sent Thane sprawling atop him once more. This time Thane used the barrel of the gun as a club, smashing it murderously again and again around the killer's head and face.

Thane's mind was a red blot of rage as he flailed brutally at the face of the man beneath him. And then he became aware that hands were pulling him by the shoulders and that a voice was shouting in his ears. The red madness blanked from Thane's mind.

"My God! That's plenty, Thane. That's plenty!"

The voice was Faber's.

Thane stared dully at the crimson pulp that was Harvard's face. He let the gun in his hand drop to the floor. He rose swayingly from the body of his adversary; the draining of his rage had left him weak, shaking.

Thane saw Colver, then. The massive killer was slumped in a corner to the right of the desk. His hands were clutched to his stomach, and blood seeped through the big-knuckled fingers.

"The little fat runt got him," Faber said. "Plugged him after the big guy had dropped him to the floor. My God! I thought that they wouldn't shoot if I walked in with the fat runt as a shield. My God!"

"Where did the fat one get the gun?" Thane asked.

"The big guy's second shot knocked the rod out of my right hand," Faber said. "The fat runt was already on the floor, he grabbed it up and gave his boss the works. My God! These guys got no loyalty to each other."

Thane saw Faber's right arm. It hung limply at his side, and blood dripped slowly from the sleeve to the floor. He turned and stared at Runt. The little fat man lay on one side. Crimson stained his coat above the heart where Colver's shot had entered. Runt still clutched the automatic that had been shot from Faber's hand. He was dead.

A groan from Harvard split the silence. The blond sadist's fingers were twitching but his body was motionless otherwise.

Thane walked over to the corner and looked down at Colver. The big man was still breathing, and his eyes were closed. His face was chalky, his mouth twisted in pain.

Thane picked up the telephone beside the desk. When the operator came in, he asked for the state police and an ambulance. He told the operator to check the number for the location from which he was calling.

They found Lynn in a room piled with shovels, picks, packing cases, and beam lifts. She was tied and gagged. Her eyes were wild with hysteria and relief when she saw Thane. She fainted before he was able to untie her bonds completely....

CHAPTER IX

The state police had arrived in less than twenty minutes, the ambulance five minutes after that. The troopers were swift and incredibly efficient. Colver and Harvard were both alive when they were removed from the shack.

An hour later, in the divisional state police headquarters, the tired young lieutenant put the telephone through which he had been speaking back on his desk. He looked at Thane and Lynn, who sat across from him.

"Colver is dead," he said. "They managed to get a fairly complete statement from him before he went. He confirmed everything you've both told me. Faber has had his hand dressed and will be here in a patrol car in a few minutes. I guess that ends it."

"What about the blond with the pug nose?" Thane asked.

The young lieutenant smiled faintly.

"Did he have a pug nose?" he asked. "I imagine it will be considerably more pugged when his face heals up."

"Then he'll live?" Thane asked.

"Unfortunately for him, yes," the young lieutenant said. "I imagine we'll turn him over to the Feds as soon as possible. The check we made on his prints revealed an astonishing background. He was German born, but educated at Oxford and several of our best eastern universities. He returned to this country from Germany in 1934, under an alias, shed that identification, and lived here posing as an American citizen from that time on. He was a band leader in the east until '37, then dropped out of that picture after a nasty riot in New Jersey. His connection with Nazi espionage circles had never been certain, but I imagine Colver's confession will bring it out of him."

"Colver knew his background?" Thane said.

"Certainly. Colver and Thurston were operating the war plant outside of Woodburn for two years. They were each slicing off a nice side graft from the substitution of equipment inferior to that specified by their government contracts. The blond Nazi agent went to work in their plant—undoubtedly under sabotage orders from Germany—about eight months ago. In two months he discovered

68

what Colver and Thurston were doing, saw the excellent chance for super sabotage, and approached Colver with his proposition. He offered him a tremendous amount of money—Nazi backed, of course —to perform out-and-out sabotage from his foolproof position as co-owner and president of the plant."

"Good God!" Thane exclaimed. "Sabotage right from the top!"

The young lieutenant nodded gravely.

"Colver went readily into the agreement, but he had Thurston to win over. He had no idea that his partner would refuse. After all, they had both been defrauding the government right along. This would be a hundred times as profitable and not greatly different. To his anger and amazement, Thurston refused." The lieutenant paused. "I imagine that Thurston's line of demarcation was reached when he realized that the money he would receive would be Nazi tainted. Peculiar reasoning, wasn't it? Some people's minds are incredible. He had defrauded his government by substituting inferior materials, and yet the unvarnished, bold-faced, naked picture of out-and-out sabotage appalled and frightened him. He made no bones about telling Colver how he felt."

"And that's when Colver decided to eliminate his partner?" Lynn asked.

"That's right," the lieutenant nodded. "He felt certain that Thurston was at the point where he would break down and go to the government with the entire story. He told this to the blond Nazi and they agreed to get him out of the way immediately. The night they decided to eliminate Thurston—last night—was premature, but necessary, since Thurston had called Colver in Woodburn that morning and told him he was going to the authorities with the entire story."

"Did he?" Thane asked.

"He didn't get the chance. Colver begged him to wait just a day, and made him promise to meet him in that tavern between five and six to talk things over. Thurston agreed, figuring he could persuade his partner to abandon the plan and turn himself over to the F.B.I. with him."

The lieutenant took a pack of cigarettes from his pocket, saw that Thane and his wife were both smoking, and shook one onto his desk. He picked it up and lighted it.

"Colver went to the blond Nazi, nicknamed Harvard, and told him of Thurston's call. They had no time to make careful or foolproof plans. They decided to get rid of Thurston first, then cover up later. The plan of drugging Thurston in the tavern, then removing him to a convenient spot to kill him, seemed good enough. Having the bartender do it would make it foolproof, since Thurston wouldn't be suspicious of any hostile scheming until Colver arrived. Colver knew that, since he and his partner had been seen together in the tavern often, he could work the joke-on-a-friend gag and get Thurston out of there easily after he was drugged."

"All of which went very well until I blundered into the picture," Thane observed.

The lieutenant smiled faintly. "And got your drinks mixed. Yes. When that happened and Thurston came out of the washroom to see you sitting on the stool he'd left, in front of his drink, he was about to point out the mistake. Then he saw that you'd finished his drink, and were drugged to the eyeballs."

"Then he must have guessed," Lynn put in.

"Of course he did," said the lieutenant. "He knew that your husband, a stranger, had finished a drink intended for him and had been knocked out by it. He didn't have to put two and two together. He knew instantly that Colver and Harvard had their sights trained on him, and that the meeting had been a stall to give them time to get him out of the picture. He was scared. He didn't know what to do. He didn't know if Colver and the Nazi killer were outside, waiting for him, or what." The lieutenant paused. "This is, of course, conjecture, but it seems reasonable enough." He frowned. "Thurston knew he had to get out of there. He knew, too, that his risk would be greater leaving alone. He seized on the plan of taking you with him, Thane, since in your drugged state you wouldn't have a great deal to say about serving as a buffer between a marked man and his hunters."

"So then he took me directly to his apartment," Thane said.

The lieutenant said, "He probably intended to leave you there as soon as he was packed and ready to leave. Colver said, in his statement to our police stenographer, that he and Harvard arrived at the apartment just as Thurston was leaving. They shot him, of course, promptly."

"Then my husband became their problem," Lynn said.

"Correct," the lieutenant declared. "He was still drugged, lying on a couch oblivious to the fact that a man had just been murdered. Colver wanted to kill him, also, but Harvard pointed out that they had an excellent opportunity to rid themselves of additional police trouble by framing Mr. Thane. They went enthusiastically to work on the job, making the wound with the poker in your husband's scalp; then planting the poker in Thurston's hand, after disposing of his bloody overcoat, suitcoat, and scarf and dressing him in his smoking jacket. They arranged the two in a position that would look obviously like struggle and murder, forced some more drugs into your husband—enough to keep him unconscious at least, they thought, ten hours more—and planted some of Thurston's money on Mr. Thane. All this took quite a little time and detailed arrangement. It was almost midnight before everything was the way they wanted it. Then they left, posting the hoodlum-foreman of Colver's, Runt, outside to watch."

Thane turned to Lynn.

"And at this time you were checking with the cab company to find out what drivers coming off work at midnight had picked up a load of a drunk and a man described as Thurston in front of the Idle Moment shortly before six. I can't get over that, Lynn. It's incredible—such detective work!" He grinned.

Lynn smiled, waving her hand airily. "It was really nothing. I found out at the bar how you had left and with what sort of a man you'd left, and at about what time. I knew drivers keep records of their loads, the addresses, I mean, and sometimes remember the description of passengers. I was positive you weren't drunk, and that it was something dreadful, since you never get to the staggeringly revolting stage when your drinking until four in the morning or so." She paused to smile maliciously at Thane. "Besides, I got the idea of checking the cab companies from a detective story I read last week. Someone did it in that. I think it was the murderer, or—no, it was—"

Thane grinned, cutting her off.

"Don't spoil the book for me, darling. I might want to read it."

The lieutenant coughed, smiled at them both, and said:

"At any rate, your wife finally had the cab people find a driver who remembered you and Thurston and came through with the address. It was almost one when she arrived at Thurston's apartment. That was when you were leaving. The two of you missed connections by minutes. You left Thurston's door unlocked and your wife went in. She saw the body, the gun, everything."

Lynn shuddered at the recollection.

"I almost lost my mind," she admitted. "I was going to bolt, to get out of there, and then I saw your letter case. It was almost out of sight in a corner of the couch. I recognized it immediately, after all, I spent enough time picking it out last Christmas."

Thane shook his head marvellingly. "Then you went to work destroying evidence, eh darling?"

"How did I know that you hadn't killed him, Dick?" Lynn protested. "After all, if my husband was going to run around killing people in such a sloppy way, I felt the least I could do was clean up after him."

"When I saw the gun and the towels in the closet I was sure the killers had placed them there," Thane said.

"That horrible blond person with the girlish voice was in the apartment after I went home with what I thought to be the evidence you'd left." Lynn shuddered. "I was certain he was going to kill me. He made me leave the towels and the gun on the floor of the closet and pack my bag with enough stuff to make it seem like I was going somewhere. Then he took some of your things, Dick. He made a telephone call, then tied me up and gagged me. After a little while that repulsive fat man appeared, and the two of them carried me out of the apartment. They had a car parked behind the building. The little fat man put me in the back of the car, on the floor, and threw a blanket over me. He left, then, and the blond with the womanly voice drove away. I didn't know where he was taking me."

"That must have been the second time I called the apartment," Thane said. "But of course there was no answer. Runt must have stayed at the apartment until I got there. Harvard, you said, stopped the car several times. He must have been telephoning Colver. On one of those calls Colver—who'd talked to Runt and realized I was in the apartment then—told Harvard to call me. Colver had the dope on the train schedules, of course, and told Harvard to use his judgment in the story he gave me to get me to go to Woodburn."

"Colver declared, in his statement," said the lieutenant, "that your untimely regaining of consciousness jinxed their frame-up. Harvard went to your apartment when they discovered your identity and finished the frame. He thought he might find something else to pick up as a plant. Lynn walked in with the gun and towels and Harvard knew she was your wife. Then he ordered her to pack, and called Colver. Colver agreed that it would be best to get Lynn out of town and told Harvard to take her to Woodburn. Colver told Harvard, too, that you'd fled the scene and might wind up at the apartment. He instructed Colver to wait until Runt arrived to take over the watch for you."

"But Faber said that Harvard came into the Idle Moment at sometime around twelve, to tell him to get out of town," Thane said.

"He probably stopped off there after leaving Thurston's apartment, on his way to your apartment," the lieutenant said. "At any rate, with your wife in their hands, they decided to eliminate you both by the car-over-the-cliff technique in Wisconsin. They figured they could frame it to look like an accident occurring on a vacation jaunt. They figured to have your clothes in the car as additional evidence. Colver bought the car in your name from a second hand place in Chicago. He drove to Woodburn in it. Thurston's body was in the trunk, and they buried him in the woods behind a summer house Colver owned off Lake Luna. My men are digging up the body now. The rest—your trip to Woodburn, being called for by Runt, and all—fits in."

"It does," Thane agreed. "But there'd have been no solution to the jigsaw if Faber hadn't come through so beautifully. He was the one element they hadn't planned on. If he hadn't arrived in Woodburn from Blufftown—where he'd gotten off the train so as not to be seen arriving with me at Woodburn—and hadn't stationed himself across the street from the hotel in a tavern to keep watch, we'd be at the bottom of Luna Lake right now."

"He told the police at the hospital that he saw Runt emerge from the hotel with you and get into the car Harvard drove up," the lieutenant said. "He followed you in the coupe he'd rented in Bluff town, driving without lights and keeping a safe distance. It's a wonder our highway patrol didn't pick him up. I'll have to give the boys hell about that—no lights." The lieutenant smiled faintly. "At any rate, he was looking over their parked sedan when Runt came out to put out the lights. He didn't seem to have much trouble with the hoodlum."

Thane grinned.

"It's easy to underestimate Faber," he said.

There was a sound in the station hallway, and Faber, followed by three state troopers, appeared at the door of the office a moment later. The moon-faced little bartender's wrist was bandaged, and supported by a sling.

"Well, well," the lieutenant grinned. "Your ears should be red, Faber."

Faber looked embarrassed. "Don't know about my ears," he said, "but my knees is, from knocking together so hard. My God! I was sure they wouldn't shoot so long's I had their pal in front of me. My God!"

* * * *

Thane, Lynn, and Faber were in the coupe the little bartender had rented, half an hour later. Thane drove, and the silence among them was that of wearily mutual agreement, each of them thankful for its

73

soothing restfulness. Lynn, her head on Thane's shoulder, was falling into a drowsy half-slumber. Faber was smoking a cigarette and staring at the dark ribbon of the highway ahead.

Faber turned, glancing at Lynn. Then, in a conspiratorial whisper, he addressed Thane.

"Say, when we get to Blufftown you can see the little lady safely to bed in the hotel there. Then I think you an' me could use a couple of stiff snorts." He sighed. "I'm off the wagon tonight."

Lynn opened her eyes and blinked at Faber.

"If there's going to be any drinking I will not be sent up to bed like a child," she said indignantly.

Thane grinned.

"I don't know if either of us should accept his invitation to a drink, darling," he said. "After all, look at the trouble caused by the last one he gave me."

Lynn sat up, her hand over her mouth in mock alarm.

"Goodness, I almost forgot about that!"

Faber's moon face crimsoned to his collar. He looked acutely distressed.

"My God!" he exclaimed. "You don't think I'd do that ag—" He choked off in horror at the thought. "My God!" he concluded with righteous indignation. "Once is enough!"

www.ingramcontent.com/pod-product-compliance
Lightning Source LLC
Chambersburg PA
CBHW020644130626
46552CB00003B/1394